DEATH ON HIGH MESA

Macey Fenner's eyes studied Ryan Tame and asked him if he had ever stood up face to face and killed a man. Ryan Tame stared balefully and said it had got to be done. The searing hatred born in him as he had watched his father shot down, his mother die flaming like a torch, and himself left for dead, renewed itself. He rode out, bitter with a vengeance that would not be satisfied until those responsible had paid in full for their horrendous deeds that bloody night on High Mesa.

Books by Elliot Long
in the Linford Western Library:

WASSALA VALLEY SHOOTOUT

ELLIOT LONG

DEATH ON HIGH MESA

Complete and Unabridged

LINFORD
Leicester

First published in Great Britain in 1991 by
Robert Hale Limited
London

First Linford Edition
published January 1994
by arrangement with
Robert Hale Limited
London

British Library CIP Data

Long, Elliot
    Death on High Mesa.—Large print ed.—
    Linford western library
    I. Title II. Series
    823.914 [F]

ISBN 0–7089–7492–9

Published by
F. A. Thorpe (Publishing) Ltd.
Anstey, Leicestershire

Set by Words & Graphics Ltd.
Anstey, Leicestershire
Printed and bound in Great Britain by
T. J. Press (Padstow) Ltd., Padstow, Cornwall

This book is printed on acid-free paper

To my wife, Pam

1

RYAN TAME could see his mother was a running, living, torch as she came screaming out of the raging orange flames of the homestead, lurid against the black night.

Horrified he reared up from the fence bottom he was sprawled against — his own suffering torn out of his mind by the horrendous sight — and gripped the corral-rail for support, a terrible anguish searing through him.

"Ma!" he bawled, his voice stark and stricken.

Desperately he turned to see Pike Benson stood nearby, as if transfixed, his hand-gripped Colt hung loosely at his side, his slack mouth agape.

In the angry light of the fire Ryan stared at the cowboy's pale, appalled, hollow face. Then Ryan's tortured gaze found Merton Pierce sat big and menacing atop his black stallion, etched in the savage glare.

"Yuh said the place was empty!" Ryan could hear Pike Benson shouting now. "God in heaven, Mr Pierce, I want no part of this!"

Ryan's tormented thoughts tore at him: weren't the murdering bastards going to do anything?

Ryan, his rage hot in him, swamped his pain. His tortured glare found Merton Pierce's craggy, stone-like face. The rancher's black eyes were mad, staring.

Ryan fought to get strength to his own shattered flesh.

But Merton Pierce's eyes still stared from under his brown ten gallon hat, glittering in the vivid conflagration, and swung from Ryan's blazing mother to stare at Pike Benson.

"Yer part of it, boy," he answered above the renewed roaring of the fire as the homestead roof collapsed in a shower of dazzling sparks behind him,

2

causing his mount to shy anxiously. "Like it or not, yer part of it."

From somewhere deep down inside him Ryan found a reckless strength, his outrage driving white-hot through him. Despite his wounds he found himself running across the ground that was steaming after the rain that afternoon, tearing off his bloody coat to meet his mother's blazing body, her tortured cries cutting him to his very soul.

Ignoring the shock of the flames licking up at him he wrapped the bloodied jacket around her. Then, before his anguished gaze she dropped to the ground on her knees, her eyes round agonised holes staring at him, the flesh of her face melting from her skull. He cried as he desperately attempted to smother the flames and quell her raking screams.

But then she became a heavy weight in his arms and gradually, through the torment of his distress, he realised she was mercifully dead. And his own cries died down to a whimpering — unmindful of the pain in his own flesh, unaware of the flames still licking out from the body under his coat, eating at him.

Inexorably then, fighting down his stunned disbelief that this had happened, a slow grinding hatred started to eat into him, killing the pain of his hurts, propelling him erect to turn and face Merton Pierce.

He became aware that Pierce was talking to him, his face grim in the intense light, his eyes staring at him through the eerie, flickering red glare.

"You don't know when to lie down, do you, boy?" he rasped.

Ryan could see the rancher's Colt coming up and levelling at him but he didn't care. All he wanted was his hands around Merton Pierce's throat; to wrench the rancher's big, arrogant body out of that saddle and throttle the miserable life out of him where he stood.

Even the orange flame blossoming from the bore of Pierce's gun and

4

the thud of lead into his flesh didn't deter Ryan. He forced his legs to carry him forward so that he could reach Pierce, but, he found, oddly, the rancher seemed to be getting no nearer to him and Ryan found his legs, which he thought were moving, had become heavy and stiff and hardly able to support him.

To his left he heard Pike Benson imploring: "He's as good as dead, Mr Pierce. Nobody could live with that much lead in him. Fer God's sake leave him and let's go."

Odd sorrow came to Ryan to hear it. Pike Benson pleading for him when the dirty, lousy snake had put his name to this! And the bewildered, bitter thoughts knifed into him keen as a Bowie: *Pike, you were my friend. Why?*

Then, cutting through his misery, Ryan heard another bang; felt another jolt to his body.

He realised he was on his knees now and the night and the action was suddenly still, as if he was looking at a photograph. And he stared in turn at the lurid features of Pike Benson and Merton Pierce. As he gazed, Oddy Sewell and Grant Flett moved up out of the night from the barn Ryan knew they had set alight. And Ryan also knew they had killed his Pa down there. Then all four men grouped around him and he found they were staring curiously at him. Then, as if sick at the sight of it, Pike Benson looked away and dropped his head to his chest, shaking it sadly, slowly.

Crystal clear, Ryan could hear Benson's plea: "God forgive me."

Ryan became aware now his outraged feelings were becoming calm and peaceful and it appalled him. Became aware that an intense darkness was slowly creeping in from the periphery of his sight.

And he was allowing himself to sink into this warm weightlessness that was overwhelming him.

Red, ragged anger flared through

him. He forced raging vengeance, more vivid than the flames that illuminated the dreadful scene before him, to roar through him. Dammit, he would not submit to death! As God was his judge, he would live to wreak terrible revenge for what had been done this night.

He fought with animal desperation to stave off the fact that the faces before him were fading into the abyss of impenetrable black that was slowly seeping in on him.

With one last mighty effort he shouted, "Pierce! Benson! Sewell! Flett! I'll see you all in hell!"

Then the blackness closed in on him fully and he pitched forward.

★ ★ ★

Through his wretchedness Ryan heard the voice.

"Lie still!" it ordered.

Fighting to get his senses through the veils of brutal pain assailing him, Ryan

7

tried to make answer to the voice, but couldn't.

He struggled to see the author of the sharp request, but he realized the whole of his face and eyes were covered with bandages. Panic struck him before he began to comprehend that it must be something placed there to protect his wounds.

And the voice, though stern, was reassuring.

That this somebody was caring for him — nursing him and wasn't running scared of Merton Pierce like the rest of the settlers in the valley — relaxed him.

And Ryan vowed some way he would reward this man for his caring. If, for nothing else, he'd live to do that.

But now, despite the comforting feeling that his life was not, at that moment in jeopardy, the blistering agony of his burns made his body feel as though it had the pain of the world thrust upon it.

He croaked, "Water."

Ryan felt the cup against his lips and the cool fluid entering his mouth. He gulped hungrily. Then, perplexing him, the vessel was taken from him. With a feeble cry he craned forward to reach it again.

"Easy." The voice warned him gently. "Too much water not good for sick man now. Little bit — often."

For a moment, through the turmoil in his mind, Ryan thought he recognised the voice then relaxed, forgetting the urge to put a name to it as he felt a cool, moist cloth patting what flesh was not covered by his bandages.

And a great thankfulness broke through his distress. He sank back sobbing and felt justified as he allowed himself to drop into a pain-filled well of self-pity.

★ ★ ★

Through the first long night, when he had lain in tearing, searing agony there were periods — after some concoction his nurse had poured down his throat — when he floated in a sea of tranquillity that seemed to rock him and caress him and comfort him.

Even so time became a nightmare hardly bearable — days and nights of raging fevers and shocking pain; of tranquillity, then shivering cold. And always the man was there — patient, reassuring; administering his concoctions and salves; cooling his body and moistening his throat and lips with blessed water.

★ ★ ★

On the eleventh day he awoke calm to find the bandages were gone from his face and body and the fever had gone, too; and the pains were easing and becoming less savage.

Blinking against the strong light he stared around him. He was in a log cabin on a bunk in the far corner of it, opposite the open door. A shaft of sunlight was coming in through the glassless window. A small fire was lit in the hearth and an iron pot was simmering on it. The smell of meat stew gnawed at his stomach making him realise how ravenously hungry he was.

The aroma caused him to lift his head and he cried out with the pain that assailed him because of the move. Gasping, fighting it with angry frustration, he blocked out his hurts and sat up and looked down at his body.

He was naked. Parts of his chest and stomach was vivid, seared flesh. He had a bullet wound in his stomach, two in his chest, one in his thigh. He fingered the top of his head. There was hardly any hair there. His brown locks were, he realized slowly, singed down to the scalp.

Then the sight of his mother running out of the homestead burst in upon his still bemused mind. And he gasped and looked away, to try and dispel the searing vision.

But he couldn't help the tears that ran from his starklingly blue eyes and he balled his burnt hands into large fists, ignoring the stinging pulling of the flesh, and thumped them against the rough-hewn pine bunk, trying to drive out his frustration and grief.

Then the area of darkness that blocked out the light coming from the open door caused him to freeze, the sensation of ice grabbing his stomach. Tensed, he looked up quickly when the voice accompanied it.

"Cry, Ryan Tame then sharpen your lance. You have work to do."

Dammit, his thoughts demanded now, why hadn't he realized?

"Walking Antelope!" he blurted.

Ryan looked up to see his father's long-time friend staring at him with brown eyes. The tall, thin frame of the Hopi Indian, clad in his silver-concho decorated broadcloth suit and his tall black stetson, with the eagle feather stuck in the wampum band around it, was a pleasing sight.

Walking Antelope . . .

His Pa had told him the story of Walking Antelope only once, but it had stuck. Years ago he had recounted how he found the Hopi in the badlands, his leg broken, shot through the side and half-starved. He had taken him back to the homestead and healed him and never once asked why he had found a Hopi dying in the badlands far from his home: And because of that, Walking Antelope had never told him.

But ever since then Walking Antelope had visited the homestead, materialising from the east on his sturdy little horse, stayed a couple of days, talked long hours with Pa then rode out again. And during that time, Walking Antelope's skill with herbs and healing had become apparent. Now, Ryan knew, that the Hopi's accomplishments had saved his life.

Walking Antelope was saying, "I bury your mother, Ryan Tame, and your father, too — good friend, Jack

Tame. Walking Antelope not forget Jack Tame, nor offspring."

Ryan fumbled for words.

"You've saved my life, Walking Antelope," Ryan said simply. "I can never repay you fully for that."

Walking Antelope grunted affably. "Ryan Tame eat," he suggested, "then we talk."

They ate in companionable silence, the jackrabbit stew appetizing and welcome. Then.

"You know men who did thing at Jack Tame homestead?" Walking Antelope said when the meal was finished.

"Merton Pierce and some of his hands." Ryan's voice caught in the back of his throat. "One I even called friend — Pike Benson."

No emotion revealed itself in Walking Antelope's face. "Jack Tame told Walking Antelope he thought Pierce would be trouble when he bought out Hight Forbes and took over the Flying F," observed the calm Indian.

"As usual my friend, Jack Tame, was right."

Ryan nodded, his sadness still huge within him for the loss of his parents, and the reasons for it came running back into his memory.

Almost immediately Merton Pierce had entered the valley, Ryan recalled, and had settled in on the Flying F he had pestered his Pa to sell High Mesa. Pierce had made no secret of the fact he wanted control of the water that rushed down from the mountains to meander through High Mesa bottomland then on down into the valley to supply Flying F land.

Merton Pierce had admitted openly he felt uncomfortable about it. Said it made him feel vulnerable, dependant on High Mesa. Maybe Pa, Pierce had suggested, if he had a mind to someday, would dam it and deprive the Flying F of its main scource of water. Pierce had added pugnaciously, this was open range; sheepmen and dirt farmers didn't belong on it.

Ryan remembered his father's rage. He'd answered in a cold, quiet voice. He ran a flock of three hundred sheep on the high pastures because it was land most suited for that, he'd said. The bottomland, below High Mesa, was ideal farmland — his cereal, hay and root crops flourished there. And, he'd further asserted, what he did with his own land was his business and no damned business of Merton Pierce. And he'd farmed here for twenty years with no trouble at all. In fact, he'd added fiercely, he and Hight Forbes had been great friends and had settled the valley together.

Finally, after more insolence from Pierce, Pa had roared at him to get off his land and not come back until he had something sensible to say. And the very suggestion he would deprive a neighbour of water was a dog-blamed insult.

After that, Pierce had gone quiet and the *Indian* raids had started . . .

It soon came clear, Ryan recalled, to

both himself and his Pa, that Merton Pierce had many business connections in the county and had a great deal of influence further afield as well.

This became vividly apparent after Wilson Strong, the sheriff of Fenton for fifteen years — the town at the southern end of the valley — was beaten by Emmet Jones in the county elections, supported and put there, it was strongly rumoured, with Pierce's money. And it soon became clear the rumours had a concrete foundation. *That Emmet Jones was Merton Pierce's man.*

Then the *Indians*. One by one the farmers and small ranchers began to be killed or burnt out. Emmet Jones had fiercely argued that it *was* Indians — that it could be nobody else. Arrows had been found and they'd been seen, warpaint and all, by the few survivors there'd been, he claimed.

But his Pa had made his views abundantly clear. It was Merton Pierce, he remonstrated, who was at the back of the troubles, for he was buying up the homesteads immediately they became available, the scared settlers fearful for their families and wanting to get out.

Glibly, Pierce had claimed he was just taking advantage of an admittedly sad situation and had offered fair prices for the land. He had also retaliated by saying he had also suffered at the hands of the redskins, though he had come forward with no evidence he had.

Ryan's gut tightened. Then it had been their turn. First it had been a field of ripe wheat burned down, then they had found eighty sheep slaughtered on the uplands near High Mesa. Both he and Pa knew no Indian would kill meat for the hell of it. He'd carry it off and use it.

Oh, Emmet Jones had poked around, made noises, but it was apparent he was only going through the motions.

But, Ryan recalled, there had been a few moments of uncertainty on their own part when he and Pa had found moccasin tracks, unshod horse prints and wampum, when they had poked around on their own, but that wasn't sure-fire proof. White men could dress up as Indians.

With his Pierce-paid posse Emmet said he'd found Indian-sign around the flat-topped low mountain from which High Mesa derived its name, though the high land was falsely named, not being a true mesa.

Pa had laughed, but without humour, right in Emmet Jones' face. Said it had to be rattlesnake-low lies.

He'd argued fervently that the Indians had been quiet for years. That he was on good terms with what few Indians still remained in the mountains hereabouts and he had talked to them and they knew nothing about it and were moving stakes not wanting trouble.

Emmet Jones had spat and claimed, "You never can trust a damned Injun! They'll lie themselves blue. They is always liable to break out an' cause trouble."

Finally Merton Pierce had used his influence to have the cavalry rid the mountains of what was left of the 'Indian scum'.

No doubt now, Ryan conjectured, staring dully at the dirt floor of the cabin, the talk would be that the raid on High Mesa and the killing of his Ma and Pa had been the last desperate raid made by the Indians, like a coyote biting at its own wounds. And Pierce and his cronies would have spread enough clues around to convince any Emmet Jones-led posse.

That would be the damned lie Pierce would be filtering through the valley, he thought bitterly.

Now . . .

Ryan's gut tightened again and he stared bleakly through the cabin door. He could see the sun bright on the red canyon walls outside.

He was surprised that Merton Pierce had been in the burning party at High

Mesa. But it was obvious the rancher had expected to kill them all — Ma, Pa and himself. And, but for Walking Antelope, he would have succeeded in doing so.

"Ryan has death in his eyes," the Hopi said interrupting his thoughts.

"It shows, huh, Walking Antelope?" he breathed. "Merton Pierce an' his cowhands are goin' to hang high fer what they done. Soon as I'm fit I'll be riding into Fenton."

Walking Antelope's eyes studied him. "Walking Antelope was in Fenton two suns ago. Glad to say that nobody look upon this Hopi as bad Indian. But while there, I listen good." Walking Antelope's face became grave. "Pierce know you missing that your body wasn't found. He not take chance that perhaps coyotes took you off, which is what people are saying. He figure you alive, somewhere. I think Emmet Jones and Merton Pierce will find way to make you liar, if you go in with story Pierce burnt you out."

Ryan stared at the tall, calm Indian gazing at him with brown eyes.

"How the hell can he?" he demanded. "I saw them. I was there, remember? Look what they did to me." He stared with angry eyes at his bullet-marked and burnt bare torso before he returned his stare to the Hopi.

"Yeah," Walking Antelope grunted. "Sure, Ryan Tame. You right to think so." The Hopi spread his arms wide and looked with round eyes at Ryan. "But Pierce a coyote. A cunning man. He would claim, if you say that, you were touched in head by what happened to mother and father. Then, Ryan Tame, you would be marked man by Merton Pierce."

"Not if I get to the law," protested Ryan. "Even Emmet Jones will have to accept what his eyes see and his ears hear and the townsfolk."

"You think so, eh, son of Jack Tame?" muttered the Hopi sceptically. "Walking Antelope live longer, seen much. Money talk big thunder in *Pahaana's*[1] world. Truth not important."

"Dammit, Walking Antelope," Ryan growled insistently, "they got to believe their own eyes!"

"Eyes can he blinded by yellow metal," insisted Walking Antelope. The Hopi's hand rested gently on Ryan's arm. "Get fit, Ryan Tame, son of Jack. When you are, contact people you know and can trust — if any left."

Ryan stared at the calm, wrinkled features of Walking Antelope, at the eyes studying him with slight pleading at the back of them.

"You are still weak, Ryan Tame," the Hopi continued, as if to reinforce his advice. "Get body strong first."

Ryan felt his hot zeal quietening. Was what Walking Antelope saying right? What would he be riding into . . . ?

Things in the valley had changed.

---

[1] White man's

A man had to think hard about who he could trust, who would listen. And a man would have to be fit to meet whatever was waiting for him. Ryan was certain, now Walking Antelope had cleared his thinking.

Merton Pierce would have several ounces of lead reserved to rub him out if not from his own gun, from the guns of hired killers. Maybe some unscrupulous bounty-hunter was already out, seeking to ventilate his hide . . .

At the thought, a cold resolve built up in Ryan as his mind accepted the possible sober truth of Walking Antelope's suggestions.

Now the hate and vengeance he had sworn on his knees at High Mesa in the savage light of the fires that had burned there, was again a raw burning sore within him.

A steely resolve tightened in his gut. Dammit, Merton Pierce's empire-building must be smashed, one way or the other. The evil that he had spread through the valley must be wiped away so men could breathe clean air again.

"Can you teach me Indian ways of making war, Walking Antelope?" he said suddenly. "I'm a farmer. I know my way around a rifle for hunting meat — that is all."

The Hopi shook his head, sadness in his eyes. "Sorry, Ryan Tame. I only know the way of Hopi history and medicine. In our tribe, such as I are not warriors."

Walking Antelope raised his arms to the roof of the cabin, his wrinkled eyes gleaming in the soft light coming through the window behind him. "Waugh! The word 'Hopi' means 'peace', Ryan Tame. We are farmers, not warriors! And I carry the soul of my tribe — its history — " he tapped his forehead — "here! Therefore, war not for Walking Antelope. I will have to go back some day to teach the young men who will follow. All I can do is get the body of Ryan Tame strong so that *he* can fight."

Ryan nodded. Inconvenient though

it was it would have to do. He wanted vengeance, bloody or otherwise. And nothing would deter him from that.

He stared into the Hopi's gentle eyes. "So be it, Walking Antelope," he said. "Make me strong."

2

WALKING Antelope's cabin was in a narrow, rocky canyon fifty miles south of High Mesa.

With great patience the Hopi healed Ryan, strengthened him, forced him through a series of punishing trials that slowly built up his fire-wasted limbs and bullet-scarred torso.

It had soon dawned on Ryan just how weak and near to death he had been. And if he had gone blundering down into Fenton with his story, maybe his sanity *would* have been brought into question, as White Antelope had suggested, and his story treated with deep suspicion. Even by the few people who were not under Merton Pierce's influence.

So he toiled. Even grasping his rifle in his fire-deformed hands, he found, was a painful and sweat-raising experience and it was weeks before he could bring it up without searing pain and hit what he aimed at.

And for days, Ryan knew, the Hopi had watched with uncertainty his pathetic attempts to draw and use his Colt .45 effectively. He had never been a gun-slick. He had used it for rattlers and little else. He had rarely worn his sixgun. And now the drawn flesh of his fire-damaged right hand made his efforts even more clumsy and slow.

Then one evening, a month later, Walking Antelope sat and stared into the fire dying in the cabin grate. "Ryan Tame struggling," he grunted. "Not shaping up like warrior."

His narrowed brown eyes studied him shrewdly. "I know man, son of Jack Tame," he said quietly after moments of thoughtful silence, "who will teach you way to use side-gun."

The Hopi made a kind of Indian greeting sign with his arm, though it appeared to indicate something far away. "He live deep in mountains, this man," he said. He grinned, showing strong teeth and stood up, the last rays of the sun coming in through the cabin window lighting his seamed face. "Waugh! Macey Fenner and Walking Antelope go way back," he boasted then, as if he had found the answer to a profound question.

Ryan gasped with disbelief, roused from his lethargy. "Macey Fenner, the gunfighter? . . . The story was he was killed years ago down on the border. El Paso, so I heard."

Walking Antelope nodded slowly, his dark face grave. "That was the story. But this Indian know different. Let us say Macey Fenner owes Walking Antelope one to help Jack Tame's son."

"*Owes you one*, Walking Antelope?" Ryan probed. "One what?"

"Favour," said the calm Indian. "The reason why Macey Fenner alive is Walking Antelope. I found Fenner gunshot, like son of Jack Tame. And when gunfighter healed, he told me he wished to live peaceful life. He wanted no more part in killing foolish young men who think they better than Macey Fenner. This Hopi understand that, too. So Walking Antelope help Fenner do that. Waugh!"

Incredulous, Ryan gasped, "Do you figure he will help me?"

Walking Antelope grinned again. "Sure," said the Indian confidently. "Like I say, we go way back. Macey Fenner not let Walking Antelope down, choose what."

Ryan eased back onto his bunk and gazed at the poles supporting the sod roof above him and thought: I'll be damned!

Next morning Walking Antelope moved out towards the big blue peaks on the other side of the semi-desert that stretched out beyond the canyons.

"One week," the Indian grunted, "then return."

★ ★ ★

30

The Hopi was as good as his word. In the meantime, Ryan had worked his hands on the smooth round rocks Walking Antelope had given him to use, squeezing them every free moment he had.

And by the day, his grip became stronger until he could use his rifle with greater accuracy than he had ever dreamed of before, the kick into his shoulder no longer troubling his swiftly healing wound there.

Now Ryan watched the two men winding their way up the box canyon Walking Antelope lived in, dwarfed by the orange, towering walls each side of them. Walking Antelope's cabin stood at the north end of it, hidden in a shallow dip until a man was almost on top of it, screened by the yucca and paloverde that had somehow found their way down here.

Macey Fenner was a tall, painfully thin man with a gaunt, square-chinned face and piercing grey-blue eyes. His dress was black, sober broadcloth and a heavy silver watch chain embraced his waistcoat. At his hip was a Walker Colt, the handle smooth and telling of once frequent use, pouched in a pliable, oiled holster. His tall ten-gallon hat perched precisely straight on his narrow head and iron-grey hair curled from underneath it.

He eased, cat-like, out of the saddle of his grey quarter horse and patted dust off his jacket, his cold grey eyes studying Ryan from their pouched sockets.

Walking Antelope dismounted and grinned triumphantly. "Like I said, Ryan Tame — Macey Fenner! Heap big gunfighter!"

Feeling slightly awed, Ryan stepped forward and extended his hand, hardly knowing how to address such a fabulous figure. "Howdy, Mr Fenner," he said eagerly. "Guess you're a legend in these parts."

Macey Fenner's gaze was neutral. "Howdy, son," he said, his voice soft, hardly above a whisper. He took the hand, then held it and examined the scarred flesh and grunted, returning his stare to Ryan's blue gaze, but not commenting on the ravaged flesh.

Then he sighed. "I sure don't feel like a legend, boy," he said. A suggestion of a smile lit up his narrow face.

At a loss as to how to talk to a man already established in the folklore of the West Ryan said, "I git some jack-rabbit stew simmerin'."

Ryan watched smiles come to both men's faces as they took reins and led their horses up to the lodgepole pine corral behind the cabin. Ryan walked with them.

"Thet sounds good to me," Fenner said. "But I'll see to my hoss first," he added, "if you don't mind."

* * *

After the meal, Macey Fenner eased back against the cabin wall, after he had found a more comfortable position on the bench seat against it.

"Walking Antelope explained your

troubles, son," he began. "You aim to kill the varmints troubling you, either with a sheriffs rope or your own gun. Thet it?"

Ryan nodded. "There's no other way in my book," he asserted, "for what they did to my Ma an' Pa. No other way."

Macey Fenner's steely eyes studied him. "You ever kill a man, boy?" he prompted. "I mean, stood up face to face and killed a man?"

A quibble of excitement bit at Ryan's stomach, together with uncertainty and anxiety that Macey Fenner might turn him down. "No, sir," he admitted. "Never have."

"So what do you aim to do?" Macey pursued. "Ambush — back-shoot?"

Ryan found the suggestion disgusted him. "Hell, no, Mr Fenner," he snorted. "I aim to meet them, one by one, stare them straight in the eye. I want them to see my face as they are gunned down."

"Thet's easier said than done, son,"

advised Fenner. "It takes a different breed to hoist a gun, stand face-to-face and pull a trigger with the intention of killing a man."

The ice-cold hatred, fired in him as he had watched the flesh melting off his mother's face, crept into Ryan. "It's got to be done and done by me." His voice grated harshly, surprising him with the venom in it.

Fenner's gaze still held Ryan's stare, steely and calculating. "How fast are you?"

Truthfully, Ryan admitted: "I don't know. Ain't ever seen a gunfight, let alone been in one. Nothin' to gauge against."

Fenner rose from the bench and pulled out a short pipe from his coat pocket. He filled it with dark tobacco and patiently ignited it with a spar of timber from the fire. When it was kindled satisfactorily he nodded his gaunt head, indicating to Ryan to join him outdoors.

Ryan rose, puzzled.

"Bring your rig, boy," ordered Fenner. "We'll find out."

Outside Ryan turned dubiously to face Macey Fenner.

"Is your piece loaded?" Fenner demanded.

"Yes, sir."

"Then unload it. We don't want accidents."

Nerves tingling within him now, Ryan did as he was bid.

When he had finished and re-introduced his Colt to leather, Fenner said quietly, "Okay, son, when you're ready."

Ryan licked his lips. "Draw you mean?"

Fenner nodded. "Beat me out of leather, boy," he whispered.

Ryan noticed that Fenner had almost inperceptibly gone quiet and had surrounded himself in a cloak of intense concentration. His grey-blue eyes watched him — cold, stern and deadly, the pipe in the corner of his mouth forgotten.

Ryan went for his piece with all the speed he could muster. And blinked as he looked at the big bore of Fenner's Walker Colt staring straight at his midriff before he had even got his hand around his own .45.

A mirthless smile played on Fenner's thin lips. "And I've lost speed, son," he said. "An' I'll tell you now I never was the fastest."

A spike of anger at being beaten so comprehensively pricked Ryan. He snapped, "Then why are you still here? Shouldn't you be dead?"

The thin, mirthless smile still stayed on the gunfighter's lips. "I shot the straightest, boy. I always had one thing concentrated in my mind when I threw down on a man to kill him." The gunfighter's steely eyes probed his own. Ryan felt his flesh creep and go chill. "Not hurt," Fenner repeated softly, "*kill*. And I let them know that just before the draw."

The anger in Ryan dispersed and was replaced with despair. "I could never match a draw like that," he said. "Never."

Fenner nodded. "No, I don't think you will," he agreed. "But the men you face will be amateurs, too."

"They say Oddy Sewell is a fast man with a gun," Ryan challenged Fenner's presumption. "They say Merton Pierce hired him for that."

Fenner's face grew serious and he puffed on his pipe thoughtfully. "Then, boy, we've got work to do. And tomorrow we start to do it." Ryan found Fenner was remorseless in his instruction. Draw. Aim. Shoot. It had to be one fluid movement. Week in, week out.

Draw. Aim. Shoot. Monotonously. Draw. Aim. Shoot.

And they had moved deeper into the badlands so their shooting would hopefully not be heard.

A bunch of Apaches showed one day, sat on a high ridge, studied them a while, then faded away.

Three months passed before Fenner

said, "Thet's it, boy. Ain't nothin' else I can teach you. Now you got to find out if you can kill a man coldly and efficiently. And God help you from here on, because I can't."

Elated at the news, Ryan prepared himself as Fenner had taught him. He calmed down, cloaked himself in the icy concentration Fenner claimed was needed. He brought his Colt out of leather, clean and swift. The pine-log target was Merton Pierce's head and three slugs hit within a card thickness of each other, plumb centre of the rancher's forehead.

"Waugh!" declared Walking Antelope.

Ryan was disappointed when Fenner was less enthusiastic. "Remember," he said grimly. "Calm. Cold. Clinical. No emotion. You're ridding vermin, boy. When you've done, put the piece away and go back to your farming. You'll live to regret it if you don't."

Ryan turned to the aged gunfighter, gratitude strong within him. He held the narrow, cold eyes that tied in with his own bright blue stare. "I don't know how to thank you, Mr Fenner," he declared.

The gunfighter's long, gaunt face was totally unemotional. "What have I done, boy?" he demanded. "Taught you how to kill . . . Do you think I'm proud of that?"

Ryan felt deflated by the gunfighter's apparent total lack of feeling for the fruits of his labour. "Then why have you done it, Mr Fenner?" he demanded.

Macey Fenner straightened his tall, thin frame, his gaze never leaving Ryan's. "Because I was asked by a friend, is all. I accepted his judgement you can handle it . . . And that you would put your gun away when the job is done."

"You talked of that before you came?" asked Ryan incredulously.

"I wouldn't have come otherwise, boy." Fenner's statement was blunt, frank and honest, Ryan clearly read that.

"Well, I'm damned!" he said.

"I hope not, boy," the gunfighter said, clear concern on his features. "*That* I *sincerely* hope."

With that, Fenner turned to Walking Antelope. "I figure to eat, friend," he said, "then ride on."

Walking Antelope grunted and walked to the make-shift camp they'd lived in for the past weeks. "I hear you, Macey Fenner."

By noon, Fenner's tall black-clad frame was a dot on the horizon and Ryan felt a part of him had gone with the taciturn gunfighter. And he and Walking Antelope left the camp that had been set up for one deadly purpose — to make himself into a killer — an hour later.

* * *

It took them two days to reach Walking Antelope's cabin in the canyon. On the fourth day after they had arrived, Ryan stared at Walking Antelope over the saddle of his chestnut mare, that Walking Antelope had brought him into the canyon on from the burnt-out hulk of his father's homestead on High Mesa . . . was it five months ago, he thought incredulously?

"If you ever need me, Walking Antelope . . . " he said.

A wry grin wrinkled the dark face of the Hopi. "Sure, Ryan, son of Jack Tame," he said, but sadness sat in the back of his eyes. "But remember what Macey Fenner say, young warrior. Put gun away when job is done. Waugh!"

Ryan nodded slowly and climbed up into the saddle. "Ain't nothin' so damned sure, Walking Antelope."

And he turned his mount towards High Mesa, grim hate and a willingness to deal death gnawing at his gut.

3

FROM where he sat atop his chestnut on the flat table edge of High Mesa, Ryan could see a cabin had already been built on the site where his father's burnt-out homestead had stood. Cold anger gripped him, sending his lust for vengeance rampaging through him with renewed vigour.

Merton Pierce had wasted no time.

He clucked at his horse and put her down the trail he'd ridden so often in a more carefree childhood and youth. No sheep grazed the uplands now, though, and no dogs ran alongside his horse.

Cattle trampled the bottomlands where the fields had been and spread like brown stains over the upper grazing lands. Must be about four-hundred head, he estimated, narrowing his eyelids, his ice-blue gaze glittering under the dark shadow of his stetson brim, his body ignoring the thrashing heat of the noon sun beating down on him.

He was almost at the cabin before the man fixing shingles on the roof became aware he was there. Ryan recognised him as being Jolly Sims, one of Merton Pierce's hands. His name did not betray his character. Ryan knew him to be a sour man who talked little, but was straight enough.

"What are you doing on my land?" he demanded. Jolly Sims halted halfway through the stroke of the hammer on his hand. He turned, startled and stared at him.

"Who the hell are you?" he growled. "This is Flying F land."

Ryan was momentarily surprised Sims didn't recognise him, but then he remembered the time back in the canyons when he had first gazed at the reflection of himself in the pool of water the spring made near Walking Antelope's cabin; and how he had been revolted to see his face so scarred with vivid burnt flesh, his once-handsome features almost destroyed.

Slowly recognition came into Jolly Sims' eyes.

"God almighty!" Stunned, Sims' dour-looking face lengthened. "Ryan Tame! They said the Injuns had taken you off, or coyotes. My God, boy, you're a mess."

Ryan quelled his anger and hate. His quarrel wasn't with Jolly Sims.

"Seems they were wrong, don't it?"

Sims edged down the roof and climbed down the ladder to stand and stare at Ryan, who sat motionless astride his horse on the trodden ground before the cabin.

"What the hell happens now?" Sims, a trifle bewildered, demanded. "Merton Pierce is supposed to have bought up this land after no relations of your'n could be found. This here's a Flyin' F line cabin now."

Ryan eased his weight into a slightly

45

more comfortable position in the saddle and studied the waddy coldly.

"I think not, Sims," Ryan said quietly. "It's my land. And when you ride off it to tell Merton Pierce, tell him I'm going to see Sheriff Jones in Fenton and acquaint him with who murdered my mother and father and near did fer me as well."

Sims frowned and his slightly blood-shot eyes eyes narrowed. "*Who* murdered yore kin? What you mean; son? Twas Injuns, plain as day," he asserted. "I was with the posse thet came out here when the glow of your burning house had been seen thet night. Red varmint sign was everywhere."

Ryan set his chin grimly. "It was Merton Pierce, Oddy Sewell, Grant Flett and Pike Benson," he informed coldly and watched the puncher's face twist up with disbelief for a moment.

Then Sims glared. "You out of your mind?" he breathed. "God dammit, your ordeal has flipped you, son." He blinked owlish eyes. "An' Pike Benson, you say? Thought he was a friend of your'n?"

"Yeah. He was." Ryan's reply was cold, bleak.

Sims stared at him now. The waddy seemed uncertain, as if he was thrown into confusion and indecision. Then he gestured with a gnarled hand. "Pike's dead," he informed flatly then. "Ain't you heard?"

The news stunned Ryan. He stared at Sims. "How?" he demanded.

The waddy went on now, as if eager to break the news: "He was gunned down three weeks ago while he looked for strays in the badlands to the south . . . Nobody knows who done it."

The news hit Ryan brutally. Strangely, though, he felt relieved that the need to get his one-time friend had been removed. "Shot down?" he demanded. "Pike . . . ?"

Sims nodded, then stared at Ryan, his eyes full of warning. "Son," he advised, his voice hardening, "you'd better not say what you just said to me in town. They'll think, as I think now, you've been tetched stupid by your ordeal. It's well known your father and Merton Pierce didn't see eye to eye."

Then Sims' eyes narrowed suspiciously. "God almighty, Ryan," he muttered incredulously, "*you* didn't gun down Pike, did you?"

Anger burned in Ryan. "Now *you're* touched," he growled. "Though I'd have had cause enough." Then Ryan narrowed his eyes. He looked bleakly at the puncher. "You say you were in the posse thet rode to High Mesa?"

Sims nodded vigorously.

Ice bound Ryan's stomach. "Then you saw my mother . . . "

Sims' face lengthened and his eyes saddened and avoided Ryan's own direct stare.

Then the puncher nodded, his face long. "It must have been terrible fer you, son," he muttered quietly. "An' it was proved it was your coat thet smothered the flames. It had two or three bullet holes in it an' a deal of blood soaked it. It was plain to see you'd tried to save her before they git you. We left thet Hopi, Walkin' Antelope, to do the buryin'. He insisted."

Sims screwed up his eyes now against the glare of the noon sun. "What did happen to you? Where did you go?"

"Merton Pierce gunned me down," Ryan stated baldly, watching for Sims' reaction. And Ryan didn't feel the need to tell of Walking Antelope's part in it. "The rest I ain't tellin'."

Sims glared. "Damn it, what you say's got to be lies," he insisted adamantly. "The four men you named were all in Fenton playin' cards in the back room of Wallace Bar that night. Chuck Shannon, the barkeep, swore to it."

Ryan snarled through thin, grim lips: "Chuck Shannon could be in Pierce's pocket."

Sims sighed and shrugged and nodded in half-agreement. "Well, I ain't arguin' with you on that," he said. He looked up at Ryan, then spat. "Okay. I'll take your message. You can deal with it yourself from there. Though I'll give it to you straight, boy. If you go into town with thet story, it'll be a straight jacket fer sure."

"Pike Benson," Ryan started. He stared at the puncher, ignoring his friendly warning, remembering — despite his feelings of hate for Benson now — his former friend's distress to see his mother's blazing body that dreadful night. "He say anythin' between the burning of High Mesa and him getting shot?"

Sims looked puzzled and shuffled his feet. "Like what?"

"Hints . . . that maybe it wasn't Injuns thet fired High Mesa?"

"Dammit," growled Sims his dour face long. "Was he likely to say thet if what you say was true?"

Then Sims' stare gripped Ryan's own. Ryan watched sudden doubt enter the waddy's face for the first time.

"Come to think of it," he said

putting his hand thoughtfully to his mouth, "Pike did go kinda quiet after the burn-out of your place."

Sims' grey eyes still held his own. "I thought maybe it was because of you being assumed dead and thet he was kinda sad about it."

Sims shook his head. "But it kept on," he continued. "He seemed to retreat into himself. Change completely. And he had one hell of a row with Mr Pierce, too, three weeks back. Most of the boys thought he'd be sacked. But he was kept on. Then, two days later, he was found shot down."

Sims blinked up at him, half-enlightenment on his face. "Now, son, come to think of it, thet was a mite suspicious . . . "

Then the puncher's face altered to sheer disbelief. "Naw . . . Can't be. Dammit, Merton Pierce went near crazy about the killin' of a Flyin' F hand. Put up a thousand dollars reward for the killer dead or alive. Had half the Flyin' F bunkhouse and the whole of Fenton out lookin' fer the damned varmint that did it. I was in it myself."

"A front," growled Ryan. "Was the killer ever caught?"

Sims looked thoughtfully at Ryan for a moment before shaking his head determinedly. "No," he grunted, "I ain't buyin' it. You've git yourself a little twisted in the mind, boy."

Ryan climbed down off his chestnut mare and ground-hitched her. "Get off my land, Sims," he said quietly. "And deliver my message. That's all I ask of you."

Sims' look was almost pleading as it met Ryan's. "Think about it, boy," he urged. "Save yourself a whole lot of grief."

"When the killers of my Ma and Pa are brought to book," Ryan gritted, "then my grief will be laid to rest, Sims. *Adios*."

Sims paused, opened his mouth as if to say more, then shrugged his shoulders. "Suit yourself, Ryan," he said. "I've said my piece." He touched the brim of his black stetson. "S'long."

Ryan watched the tall, gangling sour-faced puncher walk bow-leggedly to his bay horse held in the corral near the river. Ryan stood motionless as Sims rode back up the slope towards him.

Then Ryan drew his Colt and turned with fluid speed and blasted three shots within half an inch of each other into the door of the cabin which had suddenly become, in Ryan's imagination, the face of Merton Pierce.

Then he quickly reloaded the gun, watching as Sims stopped his horse, stared at him with narrowed eyes, his hand poised over his own piece.

For the puncher's benefit, and to give Merton Pierce more to think about, Ryan cased his Colt and allowed a mirthless smile to twist his scarred lips before he drew his piece again with blurring speed and re-cased it within the time of two eye-blinks.

Then, with deadly calm, he instructed

bleakly, "Tell Pierce that, too, Sims."

Obviously impressed Sims nodded. "You got it, boy," he grunted. "Sure is eloquent. I guess there's more than a little trouble about to visit this range. An' I don't want no part of it."

4

THAT afternoon Ryan circled the Pierce herd grazing his land, waving his blanket and shooting his gun. It took little time to get the herd running east, as far away from Flying F range — which was west — as possible.

Then he made his camp atop of High Mesa and waited. And he didn't have to wait long for his bait to bear fruit. Sims had been quick to take his message to the Flying F.

Just after sun-up the following day three riders came in from the west and circled the cabin.

Ryan put his fieldglasses to his narrowed eyes and scrutinised the horsemen. Each mount wore the Flying F brand. Two men he didn't know; but the tall, thin hombre with the fine blond hair hanging to his shoulders from under the low-crowned black stetson, he did know. Oddy Sewell.

Merton Pierce was wasting no time, Ryan thought grimly.

The riders circled for some time before they got brave enough to halt in front of the line cabin and dismount.

Then Oddy Sewell hefted his long-barrelled Colt and kicked the loose door open.

Ryan adjusted the fieldglasses to make the focus even more sharp. He watched Sewell enter the cabin. After moments he came out, inspected the three bullet holes Ryan had put in the door yesterday noon, then turned looking suspiciously around the undulating bottomland. Slowly his gaze worked round to the top of High Mesa.

It made Ryan slightly uneasy to stare back at Oddy Sewell. The gunslinger seemed to be looking straight at him before his gaze moved on. Then the three of them started talking amongst themselves and gesticulating.

Ryan eased back from the lip of High Mesa. He cased his fieldglasses and pushed them into his saddlebags, secured across the chestnut's rump. Now to really let them know he was around, he thought grimly.

He swung up onto the back of the big mare and urged her into a looping run to the west, below the horizon. The ground was dry and hard but was knitted together with brown grass and there was little dust.

He came upon the thin trail to Fenton from High Mesa an hour later — which afterwards carried on to the Flying F — some six miles from the cabin. Topping the bluff rearing above the road he dismounted again and drew his fieldglasses. The trail was still. The heat from the morning sun was already building up and dancing on the horizon to threaten another burning hot day.

After two hours he began to think he was too late — that Oddy Sewell and the other two riders had swung their mounts and headed straight back to the Flying F, or Fenton, without even scouting out the land around the line cabin and must have been well down trail before he had arrived here.

He cursed softly under his breath.

But the click of gun-metal in his ear and the cold bore jamming into his neck was sudden proof he had miscalculated.

"Freeze you dirt-eating bastard," a voice ordered.

Ryan became very still. Hands roughly grasped him then. The two waddies hauled him to his feet, spun him round and relieved him of his Colt and fieldglasses. Ryan stared into Oddy Sewell's grinning face, at his one grey eye and one brown one. The gunfighter's teeth were dirty and crooked.

Then Sewell's gloved hand slashed across his face with stinging force, shocking Ryan into raking, quiet anger. He jerked forward against the restraining hands of the waddies.

Ryan watched Sewell's odd eyes

search his scarred face. "Hell, you're a mess, like Sims said," he grunted, his slow grin fixed. He narrowed his eyes and nodded down to the rock Ryan had been lying on. "What were you figuring to do, boy? Bushwhack us?"

Ryan blinked and subdued his anger, remembering Macey Fenner's advice to stay ice-calm.

"You'll git yours front, Sewell," he grated.

Sewell he-hawed a laugh. "Dammit, you really don't know when to lie down, do you, boy? I ain't ever met a more mule-headed man. Your daid. Don't you realise that?"

He raised his long-barrelled Colt and pointed it. Ryan stared at the big bore lined straight up on his eyes and his gut went icy cold.

"Bang!" shouted Sewell.

Ryan flinched, a spasm of nerves biting at his stomach. Then evil rage boiled into him as Sewell he-hawed again, seeming delighted with his little ruse.

"I'd ventilate you now," Sewell continued, when his laughter had died down, "only Mr Pierce wants to have a look at you. He really don't believe you're alive. Come to think of it, neither did I after the state we left you in that night." He grinned mirthlessly. "But, dammit, here you are! Large as life!"

Sewell stood, his slack mouth still fixed into a mirthless grin, his eyes glittering and merciless. Then he turned to the two waddies. "Tie him good, boys," he said then, dropping all levity from his voice. "This hombre's as slippy as an eel."

Ryan fought with bull strength against the two waddies and it needed a stunning blow to his head with a gun-barrel before they got him bound with a long hemp lariat. The bonds bit agonisingly into his flesh. Still wobbly, he was pushed atop his chestnut and soon all four of them were pounding trail.

To Ryan's half-surprise, though he couldn't really figure why he felt it, the three riders looped around Fenton and it was well dark by the time their mounts swaggered down the slope and halted on the bare ground before the long front verandah of the Flying F ranchhouse. Sewell and the two hands dismounted slowly, stiffly and loosely tied up their mounts. By the noise coming from the house, hands were at supper.

"Ho, in there!" Sewell bawled.

Ryan ached in every muscle and his head throbbed where the gun barrel had striped him. The effort he had had to put into staying atop his mount left his legs, now he relaxed them from gripping the horse's flanks, numb and shivering.

The noise inside the ranchhouse dropped. Ryan's gut froze when Merton Pierce came through the wide door out onto the verandah, his boots ringing hollowly on the boards. He was at the head of some twenty hands. Ryan watched the frown on the rancher's rugged, grooved face clear and his coal-black eyes come alive in their layers of lined fat.

"Well . . . You've done it, Sewell," he breathed. "By God, he *is* alive."

Pierce stepped down from the verandah and waved a big, brawny arm. "Haul him off thet horse, boys," he ordered.

Three hands hopped gleefully down the steps and Ryan grunted as they tugged him out of the saddle. His numbed legs let him down immediately he hit ground.

"Pick him up!" demanded Pierce.

Unceremoniously, Ryan felt himself being hauled upright again. This time, wincing at the great pain as blood returned to his numbed limbs, Ryan stayed erect and glowered at his tormentors.

Pierce turned and addressed the ranch-hands gathered around. "I bet a sack full of gold eagles this is the *hombre* thet did fer Pike Benson," he said. "I bet he's been skulking round fer weeks waiting to pick us all off, one by one. Like Sims said he must be tetched in the head to think it was me an' Benson an' Sewell an' Flett thet burned out the High Mesa an' it's made him as mad as a rabid dog. But thet ain't goin' to bar him from justice bein' done. A man, crazy or not, ain't no call to go around pickin' people off from ambush without a shred of evidence."

Ryan glared at the elated rancher, enraged by the suggestion. "That's a damned lie," he grated. "You killed my Ma and Pa and damn near killed me. But when you get yours, and you will, it'll be front. I'm no back-shooter. And my bet is you killed Pike Benson, too."

Pierce looked around the faces, now lit with handheld oil-lamps. He crowed mockingly, "Like Sims said the man's plumb crazy." His eyes glittered as they returned to stare at Ryan. "It's been proved positive we were all in the Wallace Bar when the Indians razed High Mesa. And I was on business elsewhere when Pike got his. What you got to say to thet, Tame?"

Ryan straightened. Slowly he brought his blue stare to meet Pierce's mocking coal-black glare. Now he figured it would be fruitless to try and defend himself here. Probably most of the waddies on the Flying F payroll did not know what had been going on; that it had been Pierce, Flett, Sewell and Benson and maybe one or two others that had caused the mayhem in the valley, unbeknown to them. The rest of the hands would have been conditioned into believing it was Indians and that would be what they would likely accept. Ryan felt he could bet money on it. It went with loyalty to the brand.

But Ryan felt his anger eating into his soul at Pierce's confidence. Almost quivering with frustration he fought to come in line with Macey Fenner's much expressed dictum back in the badlands: to calm himself and to tell a man he was going to die and keep telling him.

"You're a dead man, Pierce," he said, almost as a whisper. "I'm going to kill you. Believe it."

Disbelief came to Pierce's eyes. "God you've got gall, Tame," he growled. "You're goin' to be strung up, you hear? This ain't no damned picnic you're on."

He turned to the grouped Flying F riders behind him. "Ain't thet right, boys? Ain't thet what we do to back-shootin' scum? You-all saw what was done to poor old Pike Benson. Well, in my book this is the scum that done it. Get a damned rope."

The lynch-talk now worried Ryan. A mob could easily do it, given the right incentives, true or not. And Pierce was making sure he was providing them with plenty of encouragement.

Ryan blinked, swallowing down the dry fear that was now at the back of his throat. He glared around him at the riders, grim-faced in the yellow light. "So thet's what an upright citizen does?" he sneered then. He waved a dismissive head towards Pierce. "This pillar of society. The big man in the county. He lynchs people, trial or no trial. Jest strings them up, no qualms. Boys, I tell you hand on heart, I didn't kill Pike." He turned to Pierce, tall and rangy and menacing in the pale light, his black eyes glittering, a grin frozen to his dark features and glared.

"He did!" he proclaimed.

Now Ryan's eyes found Sewell, and his brain worked feverishly to try and see a way out of this situation, and the germ of an idea came to him. He glared at the slack-mouthed gunslinger. "Or had thet rat-faced, yellow-bellied back-shooter do it," he growled fiercely.

Sewell's eyes narrowed and outrage froze his face into a mask of disbelief before bright anger released it.

"*What?*" he growled menacingly.

Ryan watched Sewell begin to tremble visibly. "You talk a big fight, dirt farmer," the gunslinger hissed evilly. "Sims said you were fast — how fast? Because now you gotta prove it."

With blurring speed Sewell drew, bringing up the long-barrelled Colt to cause Ryan to stare down into its black-eyed bore.

"Well, dirt farmer?" demanded Sewell.

Ryan felt a tremor of panic grabbing at his gut for a moment. Sewell was fast. Damned fast . . .

But then satisfaction that his ruse might be working swamped his disquiet. Was this to be his baptism? His meeting with destiny? The act that would stamp him a killer whether it was for good, or evil? Macey Fenner had said it: You either had it, or you didn't and you'd never know if you didn't . . .

"Like I said, Sewell," he mouthed bleakly. "You're a no-good, low-bellied back-shooter. If I had a gun, there would be only one thing I would do — *kill you*."

Ryan calmed himself down; settled into the deadly, concentrated posture Macey Fenner had instilled in him, week in week out in the badlands, focusing himself on Sewell to the exclusion of all else. Nothing remained around him. There was only Sewell before him, the gunslinger's odd eyes wide with disbelief and fury.

Then Ryan saw Sewell's eyes narrow; uncertainty seemed to cross his features and Ryan's cold iciness rejoiced silently. Fenner was right. He was destabilizing Sewell, causing doubt to come to him.

Ryan now realised that his insults had brought a reaction from the punchers gathered around, too. They turned to Sewell expectantly, their eyes demanding more than words. Insults like that would have to be answered, or a man lost credibility forever, especially a man like Sewell who made his living by the gun.

Ryan noticed a thin sheen of sweat had now formed on Sewell's forehead. The gunslinger licked his slack lips. "Cut him loose, Mr Pierce," he urged anxiously now. "He's gotta be made to eat those words. I don't take pay to accept his damned insults. 'Sides, you want him dead, don't you?"

Cunning came into Pierce's eyes. Ryan noticed it immediately, but reckoned few of the hands did.

"Well, I don't know, Oddy," the rancher said doubtfully. "I guess Tame does have a point about law an' order and using the courts to settle the business, instead of a neck-tie party. I guess it's my responsibility as a law-abiding citizen of this county to see that happens and set aside my own feelings on finding the killer of a Flyin' F hand. They could say I had you kill him in this gunplay to shut him up."

Sewell's eyes narrowed. "He done insulted me, Mr Pierce," he hissed. "Plain downright insulted me. I can't let it ride. Give him a gun."

Pierce rubbed his chin, as if deliberating profoundly on the matter within himself. "Well, I don't know, Oddy . . . "

A puncher nearby interrupted and grunted, "Sewell should have satisfaction, Mr Pierce. Them was hard words from Tame. More than any man should be expected to take."

Immediately, agreeing noises came from the bunched cowhands. That was the kind of justice they understood.

Pierce seemed to bow now, reluctantly, to their opinion. "Very well, boys," he said. "Though it don't sit well."

He sighed heavily and nodded.

"Okay," he capitulated. "Cut Tame loose and give him his rig."

Eager hands soon had the bonds off Ryan and he felt the blood flow agonisingly into his starved veins. He worked anxiously to get his limbs working efficiently and fluidly. He knew, within the next minute or so, his life would depend on their effectiveness.

Luckily, his mare had wandered off with the other horses to chew hay near the barn maybe a three hundred yards away from the ranchhouse. Ryan knew his gun-rig was in Sewell's saddlebags. He worked quietly on his limbs, all the time composing himself in the Fenner tradition instilled in him through months of gruelling work.

This was Oddy Sewell before him, one of the killers who had downed his Pa and made a torch of his mother.

Again, as in many a nightmare since that night, the stark picture came, fanning the hate he lived with. He put a loop on it, pulled it down into his subconscious. He just concentrated on Sewell, on his tall, thin figure, his straggly, fine blond hair poking out from under his flat-crowned stetson; his slack mouth and odd coloured eyes that Ryan found were now studying himself.

Ryan turned, tuned his mind to an intense concentration of cold, cruel speed and of putting lead into Oddy Sewell.

A puncher finally handed him his rig. He strapped it on. It felt comfortable and familiar.

And all the time he held Sewell's narrow stare. The gunfighter was quiet now, pale, fidgety, unsure.

"Like I said," Ryan whispered, his whole being electric and alive now as he hung his hand near his Colt, his mind concentrated on Sewell and the draw he was about to make. "You're a dead man, Sewell!"

Then Sewell was diving for gunmetal. He was coming up a micro-second in front, Ryan knew. But the ice-coolness remained in Ryan and the detonation of his own gun merged with Sewell's, melding into one horrendous, ear-splitting sound.

Ryan felt his hat snatch from his head as he sent off his second shot. But already Sewell was rigid, staring, a red hole half an inch across stamped on his forehead; brains and blood were spurting out at the back. Ryan saw his second shot hit Sewell's heart.

Sewell quivered a moment, his odd-coloured eyes quivering and staring into space. Then he collapsed as though he was a rag doll that had lost all support.

Using the stunned silence that followed, Ryan acted quickly to put the plan that had come to him just before he had challenged Sewell into final action. He grabbed the red, stringy neck of Merton Pierce and brought his Colt up to press on the rancher's temple. And thanked Walking Antelope's insistence he kept squeezing. His grip caused Pierce to scream out and his eyes bulge.

Ryan surveyed the punchers around him icily. "I'm leavin', boys," he grated. "Make one bad move and Pierce gets it."

He shook the rancher violently. "Ain't thet right?"

Pierce's black eyes were frightened and coal-black and glittering in the light of the oil-lamps as they stared at him.

"Do as he says, boys," he croaked.

Ryan could feel the rancher's vocal cords vibrating under his grip. He shoved him forward, down towards the corral, instructing the cowhands to retreat before him so he could keep his eyes on them all.

At the corral, he studied the horseflesh

in it. There was a particularly fine-looking roan. He glared at a puncher. "Put a rope on the roan and then put my rig on it," he ordered.

The waddy looked to Pierce for guidance. The rancher nodded, urgently. "Do as he says." And within three minutes the horse stood saddled and ready.

Pierce was choking. "You won't get away with this, Tame. By God, I'll see you in hell for this."

Ryan glared into the rancher's black stare. "Maybe, Pierce," he muttered. "But you'll be there first to greet me."

He turned to one of the punchers. "Get a lariat," he ordered.

The request complied with Ryan looped it over Pierce and drew it tight round his chest.

"I'll leave the chestnut in exchange," he said to nobody in particular, implying a horse-trade, not a horse-steal.

Then he swung quickly up onto the

roan's back gripping the lariat attached to Pierce. The horse was fresh and perky and Ryan was happy to feel its strong limbs under his gripping thighs.

The punchers moved back, holding their lanterns high, most looking to Merton Pierce for instructions.

"Move, Pierce," Ryan ordered then. He stared at the punchers. "Follow me and Pierce'll get it. You have my word."

"Do as he says," ordered Pierce, pale and trussed like a chicken in the weak yellow light of the lamps.

Eyeing the restive punchers seriously, Ryan put a boot into Pierce's back. "Move."

The tension was electric now throughout the crowd of riders. It was demeaning to see their boss kicked and humiliated so and having to stand there, impotent.

"Run!" Ryan demanded of Pierce as they moved into the night.

Pierce broke into a loping run, his

rangy body, clad in grey broadcloth, moving lithely. But soon he was breathing heavily and grunting. Perspiration began to run freely down his face in the close night. It wasn't long before he was showing signs of deep distress.

After four miles Ryan dropped the rope.

"Where's your gun, Pierce?" he demanded.

The rancher slowly disentangled himself from the lariat that had been around him. He was breathing heavily and ringing with sweat.

Through the dark night, relieved only by the faint glow of a thin, sickle moon, the rancher glared up at him. "I never eat with a gun on. It's back at the ranch."

Disappointment pricked at Ryan.

"Then you've got damned lucky," he growled.

The whinney of a horse cut the quiet of the range night bringing Ryan's head around immediately to locate its position. But the crack of a rifle and the hum of lead past his head had him spinning the roan and his Colt coming out of his holster to point at Pierce. But already, Pierce was running for the cover of rocks, their dark bulks hardly discernible in the pale silver light.

He snapped a shot in his direction.

5

NOW the roan reared, alarmed, before plunging into the night. Rifles were going off with more frequency now, ripping the stillness of the air with ragged noise. Ryan heard lead humming like angry bees around him. He figured the punchers — if that was who was shooting at him, and it was pretty safe to bet that it was — were throwing random shots into the darkness in the hope they would get lucky.

Then angry pain ripped through Ryan's leg and the roan shied and squealed. Ryan found the hurt now in his leg was savage and sore and he could feel wet blood already running down into his boot.

And he could hear Pierce bawling in the night, a distance behind him.

"Bring me a horse!"

A hint of desperation came to Ryan, but it comforted him to feel the smooth rhythm of the roan's stride under him. Instinct told him he had chosen a horse with speed and stamina.

He had to head for the canyons, he decided grimly. With any luck he could lose them in that tormented land. Then he would have to get his leg attended to.

Walking Antelope sprung immediately to mind. But he didn't want to implicate the Hopi any more in his troubles. He owed the Indian more than he could ever hope to repay now.

He tugged away his bandana from around his neck now. It was dirty with the dust of three days travelling, but that could not be helped. He had to do something about his leg.

Fighting against the jogging of the running horse beneath him, he managed to fashion a rude tourniquet and was gratified to see the blood oozing through the hole in his levis from the wound was slowing to a dribble, though aggravated by the motion of the horse. It was then, in the gloom, he noticed the horse had suffered a graze from the bullet as well. So that was what had made the animal squeal.

★ ★ ★

By dawn he was close to entering the twisted landscape of the canyons and paused atop a rising butte, keeping just below the skyline. He was weak in the saddle. He stared at the golden sun lipping the horizon east, spearing shafts of sunlight across at him, tinting the orange, angry land before him with stark light.

Then he studied the undulating brown-green landscape he had just ridden through — still ribbed with dark in the hollows — slowly becoming arid scrub, then melding into the barren wastes of the beginnings of canyon country.

It had been a long, desperate night. He had paused only long enough to pull out his clean, spare cotton shirt and make crude bandages of it. Then he had loosened the tourniquet for the final time, dropped his levis and bound the bullet wound in his thigh, figuring it had bled long enough to perhaps avoid the dreadful possibility of gangrene.

Now he was tired, hungry and fearful for his life. And also, on reflection, and it was no use pretending otherwise, he had gone blundering in like a wet-eared fool and he had paid the price. Now he was a hunted man and known to be very much alive. But, as a consequence, Sewell lay dead and Merton Pierce now had to live with the knowledge he had a fight on his hands.

And now, Ryan thought with a grim warmth, only Grant Flett and Merton Pierce remained to sate his need for vengeance for what had been done at High Mesa.

But he hadn't made any friends back there. Fact was, he mused, the whole of the Flying F bunkhouse was solidly behind Merton Pierce now because of the rancher's sudden and self-righteous stand against the neck-tie party. And also — the next fact came slowly to Ryan — the story would make good listening for the upright citizens of Fenton. And his own deliberate goading of Sewell and ruthless gunning down — even though the shitbag was a murdering gunslinger — would be bad press.

Growling to himself and pushing his fears to the back of his mind he fumbled out his field-glasses and searched the mauve land at his rear.

Then his body became taut as his scrutiny found the bubble of rising dust, brightened rosily by the sun, moving slowly towards him. Under the pall were the dark blobs of riders. And they were maybe five miles in his rear, he reckoned.

That Pierce was ruthless, he knew, but he hadn't anticipated such determined tenacity. He had, perhaps naively, figured that maybe Pierce would give up the chase and seek bounty hunters to do his work. Ryan sighed. Looked as though he'd figured wrong, again.

He cursed his impetuosity and naivety. Pa had always said it would get him into lots of trouble he'd be well without until he learned to curb it.

But now . . . His thoughts pondered his next strategy. He would have to try and use the horse sympathetically. It was his only ticket to getting shuck of the punchers behind him.

He cased his field-glasses and turned the roan towards the canyons. He knew there was a cap of hard, bare rock maybe four miles ahead of him that extended for miles south. If he could get to that, he would maybe shake the tenacious posse behind him. Then he would be able to rest up and heal up and get rid of this awful tiredness that was bugging him.

As the sun rose higher, his lassitude became greater. He chewed jerkily and sipped water sparingly. And it comforted him to listen to the clop of his mount's hooves on the rock he had been making for. That should throw them, he thought wearily.

Finally he came off the rock and sidled down into a deep canyon and splashed into the stream running lazily in its bottom. They wouldn't know, if they ever got to here, whether he had gone east or west now. The thought comforted him.

By early afternoon he had left the canyon and was surprised to find himself moving out, with the stream, into grassland. This was country new to him. He had worked the canyons and badlands mostly to the east and he knew he had been travelling south most of the day.

He found his fatigue was great now, aggravated, he figured, by his loss of blood and the fact that he had not slept for almost three days. He had to rest and the horse did, he decided. He had asked much of it, but it had risen to his demands nobly.

With tired eyes, that felt as though they had hot sand at the back of them, he studied the oasis of green he had stumbled upon. About a quarter of a mile up-stream was a clump of willow and cottonwoods. They looked inviting.

He could maybe risk a hot meal and a few hours sleep.

He reckoned he had shaken the Flying F hands long ago.

He moved into the cottonwoods and gathered dry sticks and thumbed a sulphur match into life.

An hour later he leaned back against a cottonwood bole and picked fatback strands out of his strong, straight teeth with the match stub he had sharpened to a point with his clasp-knife and studied the roan cropping grass contentedly nearby, secured by a long rope. He had cleaned the crease the mare had suffered. It wasn't serious, but, judging from her tantrums when he had tended it, was sore. He felt comforted. That was one fine horse he had picked out.

Now he became more aware of the throbbing and aching in his leg and it irritated him. A damned lucky shot was all it was! And it was giving him all this grief! Damn it! Damn the Flying F!

He let his sudden rage subside. It didn't help anything, but it eased his own frustration some. And though his body clamoured for sleep, he'd heard it was right to try and keep a wound as clean as possible, so he hobbled to the stream dropped his levis and unwrapped the bandage.

Around it was yellow, bruised flesh, but the actual wound itself looked clean enough and the lead had passed straight through the fleshy part at the back of the thigh.

Gently, he bathed it and rinsed the strips of shirt he used to bind it. He would have to get to a doctor, he told himself wearily. Soon as the chance came . . .

★ ★ ★

The whinny of the horse woke him.

Vaguely now he remembered edging back from the stream and pulling on his levis and leaning his back against a cottonwood, after laying out his strips of shirt to dry, then . . .

He must have dropped off to sleep. And now the horse's soft noise had woken him.

Immediately, he tensed. One thought rushed immediately into his head: The Flying F riders.

The working of a rifle lever made him go even more taut.

"What are you doing on our land, mister?"

Ryan came to his feet painfully and turned to stare at a tall, brown-haired, brown-eyed boy of about maybe twelve years of age gazing at him from under a worn grey stetson. But he held the Winchester in his hands with great assurance though, and had it pointed straight at his mid-riff.

"Passin' through, boy," Ryan said. "Jest restin' a spell."

"You belong around these parts?" the boy pursued.

Ryan met the boy's direct stare. "No, can't say I do."

Ryan felt muzzy and his leg was throbbing insistently. "Is there a town near here?" he probed. He added: "Badly in need of a doctor, son."

Ryan watched the boy's stare switch to his hurt thigh before returning to study him again.

"Basstown," the boy said. "Fifteen miles south of here."

Ryan nodded. "Heard of it," he said. He knew it to be a small mining town about seventy miles southwest of Fenton.

The boy narrowed his eyes. "You shot, mister?"

Ryan nodded. "Guess so, boy. Had myself an accident in the canyons. Damned clumsy of me." He tried a wry smile. "Takes some kind of a fool to shoot himself, eh?"

The boy nodded fervently. "Pa allus said to be careful around guns. Can't take them too seriously."

Ryan nodded. "I guess your Pa's right about thet."

And to reinforce his opinion, Ryan pointed a finger at the boy's rifle. "Speakin' of bein' careful you mind jest turnin' thet piece a little, boy?" he asked. "One accident in a day is enough."

The boy didn't comply with his request and continued to hold the rifle steadily, firmly upon him.

And Ryan looked away and noticed the sun had dipped down below the orange walls of the canyons surrounding this oasis and evening was closing in fast. Soon dark would be upon them. And he didn't blame the boy for his cautiousness. These were dangerous times.

"You live near here, boy?" he ventured.

"Half a mile up-stream."

"I'd take it kindly if your folks could

see their way to offer me a bed fer the night. A barn would do — anything, in fact."

The boy's brown gaze studied him cagily.

"Ma ain't allus happy to have strangers hangin' around."

"I could pay, son," offered Ryan.

The boy appeared resentful of that. "Ma wouldn't take too kindly to thet, either," he asserted. "She says folks should be hospitable."

Ryan looked at the boy steadily. "If thet's what she said," he grunted. "How about it?"

The boy shook his head doubtfully. "I don't know." He hesitated, a frown creasing his young brow. "I truly don't. Maybe I should ask Ma first."

"I'd be grateful, son," Ryan said hopefully. "I've ridden me some lonely trails lately." He licked his lips. "Put it to your Pa," he suggested.

The boy's eyes dulled and he looked away, his rifle lowering. "Pa's dead, mister," he said. "Last year. Steer kicked him in the head."

Ryan felt an odd sympathy for the boy.

"Thet's too bad, boy," he said. "No way for a man to go."

The boy's brown gaze studied him further. "Your face is an awful mess, sir, all burned like thet," he said, his voice suddenly more amenable. "Kinda scared me to see it when I first saw you asleep agin thet cottonwood."

Ryan nodded. "Ain't pretty, son, I guess."

The boy blinked at him. "Figure it'll do no harm to ask Ma," he said, scuffing his toe in the river sand.

Ryan felt hot now, sweaty weak from his wounds, but hopeful as well. "No harm at all, boy," he said.

The boy hefted his rifle to his shoulder. "Okay, mister," he said. He seemed to come to a strong decision. "Could we double up on your horse?"

Ryan felt the tautness and weariness in his slacken. "Ain't no problem there, boy. I'll jest tie up this wound then we'll ride. You could be saddlin' the roan while I do it."

Unthinking Ryan dropped his levis and the boy turned away self-consciously. "You could've warned me, sir," he protested.

Ryan felt wry humour tickle him, easing his hurts for a moment. "I'll remember, boy. My apologies."

* * *

Ryan found the homestead he was taken to was a low, adobe, sod-roofed structure. He'd noted a sprinkling of cattle grazing on the ride in; maybe fifty head. Now hogs squealed in a large pen a distance from the house and chickens were cackling and scratching around the bare space between the out-buildings. A vegetable plot, fenced in with chicken-wire, showed crops growing to the rear of the homestead.

The boy slid off the back of the roan and hollered: "Ma!"

A tall woman, dressed in blue gingham which couldn't hide the natural elegance of her posture, came to the door. She held a kerosene-lamp high and it lit her golden hair and etched her high cheekbones starkly. She didn't look old enough to have a boy of maybe twelve or so, as Ryan had judged the boy to be.

Ryan became aware her green stare was studying his scarred face, startled for a moment, before it met his own surprised gaze. Her beauty stunned him. He gathered his aplomb quickly.

He touched his stetson brim. "Evenin', ma'am."

The woman looked self-conscious now and smoothed down her dress. She turned to the boy.

"What did I tell you about strangers?" she demanded.

The boy shrugged slim shoulders. "I figure him okay, Ma," he said earnestly.

Ryan felt he should defend the boy. "Name's Tame, ma'am," he said quickly. "Ryan Tame. I have the High Mesa place, east of Fenton. I guess the boy thought he was bein' neighbourly."

The woman remained alert and suspicious. "What brings you around these parts, Mr Tame?"

Immediately he figured that to be a sticky one for he loathed to lie, which he knew he would have to do now. How could he say what had brought him here without alarming the lady into thinking he might be a desperado of some sort? Perhaps it would have been better if the boy had not found him . . .

"I got lost in the canyons." Ryan attempted a rueful grin. "I feel ashamed to admit it, ma'am, but thet's the way of it. Then to cap it, I've gone and shot myself in the leg. I need to get to a doctor. The boy said Basstown was close." He blinked and ventured speculatively, "Maybe there's a sawbones there . . . ?" He made a gesture with his hand. "But jest now I'm tuckered. Need to rest up. The barn would do, ma'am, if it wouldn't be troublin' you too much."

"We haven't a barn. Ephriam was getting round to it, when . . . " The woman faltered.

"Your husband, ma'am?" Ryan butted in softly. "The boy did say. No way for a man to go. May I offer my condolences?"

The woman straightened and lifted her head looking as though she was still fighting her grief. Then her face relaxed slowly. "Yes, well, thank you, Mr Tame."

Her green eyes studied him, probing the dusk that separated them. "You can sleep with the boy," she decided abruptly. "He has his own room. Put your blanket on the floor."

"Thet's mighty civil of you, ma'am," he said thankfully.

"The name is Martha . . . Martha Newsom." She nodded towards the boy now stepping up to the adobe homestead. "And this is my boy, Caleb."

Tiredly, Ryan climbed off the back of the roan and favoured his wounded right leg gingerly. It would bear his weight, he knew, but not without considerable pain.

"Proud to know you both, Mrs Newsom," he said. "Have you a place for the roan?"

"There is a lean-to behind the pigsty, Mr Tame," she said. "We keep our own horse there. Grain bin there, too. The horse looks in need of it. You have ridden him hard, Mr Tame, it seems."

"Yes, ma'am," he admitted. "We've come a ways since sun-up."

Martha Newsom lowered the lamp and gave it to Caleb. "Help Mr Tame to unsaddle his horse, then take it to the lean-to," she said briskly. "Then feed and curry it."

"Thet won't be necessary, ma'am," started Ryan. "I don't want to put you folks to more trouble than need be."

"You look ill, Mr Tame," Martha

Newsom answered quickly. "Your leg seems to be troubling you some. Caleb is well used to dealing with horseflesh. And I consider it unneighbourly not to make your stay here welcome, considering your condition."

"No trouble, sir," the boy piped up, a happy grin on his face. "Glad to help. It's a fine horse. I see it has the Flyin' F brand."

Ryan's gut tightened for a moment, before he had to lie again.

"Yes, I did a trade with the owner Mr Pierce." He patted the roan's rump. "I'm proud of her."

"You got a name for her, sir?"

Again Ryan fumbled for explanations. "Ain't got around to it yet, boy." He grinned. "You figure one?"

Ryan watched as the boy studied the horse's red-and-white mixed coat. Then he grinned up at him. "She's strawberry, sir. That's got to be her name!"

Ryan smiled, feeling the movement pulling at his fire-seared facial skin.

"Strawberry it is, boy! And a damned fine name, too."

Ryan was glad to see the pride shine in the boy's face. Caleb grinned at him. "Leave Strawberry to me, sir. I'll have her spick-an'-span in a hour."

"There's a dollar in it, boy," Ryan grinned. "I reckon a man willin' to work should be paid for it. An' the name's Ryan."

With that he turned to where Martha Newsom now stood, left hand on hip, studying him. "Thet okay with you, Mrs Newsom?"

A suggestion of uncertainty shaded the pale features of the woman for a moment before it went and left her face with that special beauty Ryan increasingly found himself admiring.

"I guess that's fair, Mr Tame," she agreed. "Please, come in. Have you eaten?"

Ryan was about to say he'd had beans and fatback on the trail very recently until the aroma, as he came close to the homestead, of meat stew assailed his nostrils. "Not lately, ma'am," he lied, willingly this time.

"Then you must share our table," announced Martha Newsom.

Ryan mumbled grateful thanks and hobbled into the warm lamplight of the small, but pleasant room. A knotted deal table was set for a meal and plain, comfortable furniture was scattered about. There was fire in the stone fireplace. At her invite he sat down at the table. Within three minutes he was eating savoury stew and chewing on a hunk of freshly-baked bread and Martha Newson ate quietly across from him.

Then she said, "I would appreciate the truth, Mr Tame."

Astonished, Ryan felt his gut tighten and he looked up from his food to stare into her frank, alert green eyes.

"The truth, ma'am?" he fenced.

Her beautiful face was open, curious. "I heard some months ago High Mesa was burnt down by Indians and all the Tame family killed. The trouble in the valley up there made hot news for months in the *Basstown Gazette*. We were fearful hereabouts for a while until the cavalry cleaned the Indians out of the mountains up there."

Ryan stopped chewing on his meat. She wanted the truth? The thought niggled at him. That would be better unsaid in such fair company. Yet . . .

Again he studied her face. It was a face that was tender, yet strong in character. An astute face, but not calculating. It invited frankness and left him with the impression she would form her own opinions when the truth was known.

There were times when a man had to gamble, he studied then. He figured this had to be one of them, if only to clear his own feelings of guilt at having to lie to so decent a woman.

He held her clear gaze and blinked. "We were burned out at High Mesa, yes," he said abruptly. "By Indians? No. It was Merton Pierce, the owner of the Flyin' F and three of his hands — one a paid gunfighter. They did their killin' an' burnin' disguised as Indians."

Ryan licked his lips, the truth clamouring within him now to come out. "Pierce was hungry to own the whole valley," he growled. "Now he has it. I won't go into how I survived, but I swore vengeance upon the men that did the burning and killin' at our homestead. They came ·undisguised. No-one was to be left alive at High Mesa, I guess. You see, ma'am, pa an me had defied him, got him figured dead to rights."

Ryan blinked and studied Martha Newsom's attentive face.

"Well," he sighed, "two of the scum are already dead. One killed, or was ordered killed by Merton Pierce, because he knew too much and threatened to talk, is my guess, the other one killed last night by me."

He held her gaze directly now, wanting nothing left unsaid. "I forcibly traded my own horse for the strawberry roan I came in here on at the Flyin' F ranchhouse last night. In the process I was shot escaping from what I feared would be the lynching of me."

Now he looked down at his scarred hands and said, "Ma'am, that's the truth of it in a nutshell."

Martha Newsom sat silent for fully a minute. "The way you wear your weapon has the look of a professional gunman. Not a farmer."

"I trained five months to get that look and had the best to teach me," he admitted fully committed now to hide nothing from Martha Newsom. "I figured to do what I have to do would need that."

"Turn yourself into a killer?" declared Martha Newsom. "Couldn't you go to the law?"

"Bought and paid for by Merton Pierce."

"I only have your word for that," she countered.

"You asked for the truth, ma'am," he grunted. "Thet's it. Whether you believe it, is up to you."

She still stared at him. The gaze left him uneasy. Her green probing eyes seemed to be peeling off his skin and looking into his soul. After long moments she said,

"I always thought it funny that the Indians broke out after all those years of peaceful co-existence and didn't come this way." She got up, her look direct and satisfied now.

"Thank you, Mr Tame, for your frankness. After your meal I will look at your wound. I have had some medical experience. And please, my given name is Martha."

Ryan opened his mouth, his respect for Martha Newsom flying as high as a bald eagle, to thank her when Caleb burst in through the open door.

"Riders approaching, Ma," he blurted. "Saw them on the skyline just now, against the last of the day. A big bunch of them."

6

RYAN stood up swiftly, the sudden movement ripping pain through his wound. The Flying F, his thoughts jarred. If it was, Pierce wanted him bad, real bad. Then he narrowed his gaze as the next thought hit him: as badly as *he* wanted Pierce!

Martha Newsom's body was now stiffly erect, her face pale, her chin lifted high and proud.

She stared at the boy. "Caleb, take Mr Tame's horse into the brush," she said calmly. "Stay with it until the riders have gone."

Startled by the sudden order, Ryan turned to stare questioningly at Martha. But before he could speak, she ordered,

"In there, Mr Tame." As she said it, she pointed to the room to the rear of them. "Get under the bed."

Ryan paused for only a second,

momentarily resenting taking directions, and such decisive ones at that, from a woman. But he couldn't come up with anything better, he realized.

Without a word he turned and hobbled into the dark bedroom. It was obviously Martha Newsom's room by the frills and the faint hint of perfume that hung tantalisingly in the still air.

Without hesitation, he crawled under the bed and stilled his taut body; shallowed his breathing.

He heard noises of movement in the room where Martha was — the hem of her dress swishing across the floor, the scuff of shoes on the iron-hard earthen floor under her feet.

Then he heard the metallic sound of a rifle lever being worked. Then silence.

Ryan hardly dared to breath. In the tense, dark stillness he lay there gritting his teeth against the gnawing ache of his wounded leg. It was throbbing painfully, causing sweat to break out anew on his forehead.

At the first sound of horses and jingling harness he tightened his muscles until they were iron-hard sinews and slid out his Colt and licked his now dry lips and listened expectantly. Then the firm, clear, feminine voice came,

"Far enough! What's your business?"

Martha Newsom's demand cut the silent stillness in the house causing Ryan to tighten his grip even more firmly around the butt of his gun.

Then Ryan could not mistake Merton Pierce's harsh voice.

"No need for the gun, ma'am," he protested gruffly.

"I think there is," Martha retaliated quickly. "These are not friendly times."

Pierce's reply came tired and conciliatory. "I'm Merton Pierce, ma'am. I'm owner of the Flyin' F ranch north of here and these men are some of my crew."

Speak your piece." Martha Newsom's voice was firm, precise and direct. It belonged to a woman who had lived in the hard wilderness and had the courage it nurtured, Ryan decided.

Merton Pierce's voice was harsher now, more menacing. "Very well, ma'am, if thet's the way you want it," he grated tiredly. "We're lookin' for a murderer, name of Ryan Tame. We believe he has come through this way."

"Burn marks on his face?" Martha Newsom demanded.

A jag of nerves jolted Ryan. His stomach knotted. Damn it, his thoughts raged then, what was the woman saying? Was she now going to betray him?

Ryan heard Merton Pierce's voice become suddenly hopeful and brighter.

"Why, yes, ma'am," he said quickly. "He pass this way?"

"He came this way about three hours ago," Martha Newsom stated. "He said he got lost in the canyons — that he had a wound to his leg. He said he had shot himself and was looking for a doctor. I fed him, bandaged his wound and directed him to Basstown. That enough?"

Martha Newsom's words had at first

torn Ryan's nerves ragged. Now he realized the neat strategy of them.

Pierce's voice came back now smooth and pleased. "That's more than enough," he crowed. "How did he look, ma'am? And how long ago is it since he left?"

"He must have been gone . . . oh, two hours, maybe," she said calmly. "He looked a tired man, Mr Pierce," Martha Newsom added firmly, "And weak from his wound. His horse was reasonably fresh, though."

At that, Pierce snorted, "Yes. A Flyin' F horse, ma'am. He's a horsethief as well."

Martha's voice came soft and surprised now. "He seemed such a pleasant man. I find your accusations alarming. You will appreciate, now, Mr Pierce, why I am cautious with strangers and perhaps a little brusque."

Merton Pierce's voice came back dry and courteous now.

"Indeed so, ma'am. Well, I guess we'll be ridin' on. Again, you have been very helpful."

Ryan lay listening while the sounds of the Flying F punchers, drumming hooves and jingling harness faded off into the now dark night. Admiration for Martha Newsom welled in Ryan. A damned intelligent woman, too, as well as having grit, he decided, after that little encounter. Certainly not the bullhead he, himself, was!

Interrupting his thoughts, Martha Newsom appeared at the door of the bedroom,

"You can come out now, Mr Tame," she instructed calmly.

Wincing at the pain the need to sidle out from under the bed caused him, Ryan eventually came erect. One question burned in his mind. He put it to Martha Newsom now,

"Why, Martha? Why are you helping me?"

Her green eyes met his blue, questioning gaze calmly and held it for several moments. Before she answered, she turned and placed the long-barrelled Henry rifle she had in her right hand back in its place on the wooden pegs in the beam over the hearth.

"Eight years ago Merton Pierce cheated my husband in a land deal," she said then. "It cost my husband two thousand dollars — his life's savings and our home as well. We were made destitute."

Her gaze still held his own, now brightening as the memory came back. "Can you imagine how that hit us, Mr Tame?" she continued. "I came out to Ephriam a child bride of fourteen, from the east. And there we were with a three year old infant — our boy, Caleb, and no home. Nothing."

Her full lips compressed. "Well, from there on, our life, which was already hard, became fierce, Mr Tame, as you can perhaps imagine. It took us six years of bitter struggle to get back to where we are . . . then Ephriam . . . " Her direct look dropped. After a moment it came up again full of pain.

"Well, these things happen, I guess."

She sniffed and smiled briefly. "So, there you have it, Mr Tame," she finished bravely. "That is the reason why I have not a glimmer of respect for the name of Merton Pierce. He did not even recognise me, we — we — meant so little . . . "

Ryan felt uncomfortable as Martha Newsom faltered, obviously moved by having the memory of her husband's death renewed and being confronted by Pierce and reminded of his callousness.

Ryan rubbed at his fire-seared, square chin and shuffled awkwardly. And the deep hatred he held for Merton Pierce strengthened and grew.

When Martha Newsom recovered, she lifted her chin in the proud way Ryan had observed and admired at their first meeting.

"How Pierce swindled us, I don't know," she continued. "He had set up some form of crooked cartel. It involved several important men, Pierce at their head. Somehow, Pierce found some way to claim the land and chisel my husband out of it."

Martha Newsom's eyes now lifted. Ryan was surprised to see the cold deadliness in them. "The day I hear Merton Pierce has been killed, or jailed, Mr Tame, I will jump for joy."

Ryan, his respect and admiration for Martha Newson filling him, said, "Well, amen to that, Martha."

He shuffled his feet even more self-consciously now. He owed Martha a great deal already. And when Merton Pierce reached Basstown and found that he had not been there it could prove awkward for Martha if the rancher chose to come back this way to do some checking.

"I think it would be best if I did some travelling, Martha," he said. "And I'd be proud if you'd use my Christian name . . . Ryan. Sounds kinda more friendly."

Martha Newsom's green eyes held his blue stare for a moment. He thought he saw a regretful shadow cross them for a moment when he mentioned he was leaving, but he could have been mistaken.

"Let me dress your wound first, Ryan," she offered, making it clear in the tone of her voice she would accept no refusal.

Ryan capitulated happily, for it was very sore. "Guess I won't say no to that. Guess, too, I've got to revise plans," he added ruefully. "Do less blunderin' an' more thinkin'."

Martha smiled at him now before turning towards the kitchen. "If you would drop your levis, Ryan, I will heat water and look out some linen suitable for bandages," she said. He could detect no embarrassment was in her voice. For himself, well . . .

Ryan felt heat flush his cheeks. He didn't know his way around decent women very well. He'd only had the occasional whore in Fenton. There had once been a dark Mexican *senorita*, Carmelita, he'd taken a shine to and had thought of in terms of marriage. A pang tugged momentarily at his heart.

But she had died of pneumonia before it had got real serious. He'd rode a pretty lonely trail since then where women were concerned.

"Sure, ma'am," he grunted.

The drum of many hooves halted his fumbling hands immediately. His gut tightened and his eyes narrowed. What the hell, his startled thoughts demanded immediately?

Martha came running in from the kitchen her face pale and set. "Back into the bedroom, Ryan," she said with a calm he didn't share. "Sounds as though Pierce has forgotten something."

Indecision hustling Ryan, he finally scrambled for the bedroom again and was making ready to squirm under the low iron chassis when Pierce bawled from outside:

"Send Tame out, ma'am, or it could go bad for your boy."

Ryan heard Martha gasp and he froze.

Martha Newsom's anguished demand came starkly now, "Caleb?"

The boy's concerned voice cut the night air. "Ma!"

Ryan got to his feet again, fighting the pain from his thigh. Despite the desperation he felt, he couldn't let this go on. Pierce was ruthless. No telling what he would do.

"Comin' out, Pierce," he growled. "Leave the boy be."

A rasping laugh came from outside. "By, God, Tame," he chortled. "You got dysentery?"

That immediately set the rest of the Flying F crew bawling with laughter.

When it subsided Pierce growled, all levity gone,

"Right, toss your gun out, Tame, then walk out hands high. One bad move the boy gets it."

His insides roiling within him, Ryan unshipped his Colt and tossed it into the dark beyond the cabin door. Then, hands raised, he followed it out. His mind worked frantically to find a way out of this for Martha Newsom and her boy.

"The boy's done nothin' I didn't order him to," he rasped. "Let him go, Pierce."

Ryan blinked when he reached the dark outside. In the light coming from the windows of the cabin behind him the Flying F crew were lined up across the bare hard ground before the homestead. Merton Pierce was already off his horse. He had the struggling Caleb by the scruff of the neck. In the rancher's right hand was a levelled Navy Colt.

"I held a gun on the woman, Pierce," Ryan snarled, angry now that Caleb was being used so and at his own stupidity that had brought Martha, the boy and himself to this. "I threatened the boy I'd kill her if he didn't do what I wanted. The whole time you talked to the Newsom woman, I had a gun on her."

A slow grin broke on Pierce's face now. His coal-black eyes glittered in the yellow light. "You expect me to believe that?"

116

Ryan blinked, hate for the triumphant rancher before him rampant, but he controlled it with effort.

"It's the truth," he grated.

"The woman had a gun!" snarled Pierce. "She made a convincing effort to make us believe she'd use it."

"Empty," Ryan said. "My idea. Clever, eh?"

A scoffing laugh came from Pierce. "You ain't git thet sort of savvy," he crowed. "You is jest a dumb dirt farmer an' sheepman."

"Fooled you good, Pierce," Ryan continued, striving to keep his voice as low and controlled as possible. "Thet ain't all I'm goin' to do, either. You killed my ma an' pa, Pierce." Ryan made no effort to disguise the venom within him this time. "You gotta pay for thet."

The grin faded from Pierce's face. He glared and gripped the big weapon in his hand until the knuckles showed white.

"The sooner we get you to Fenton

and on the end of a rope the better, Tame," he grated. "An' I ain't believin' the story about the woman. In my book she aided and abetted a known killer. How does thet sit, Tame?"

Ryan's gut went ice-cold. God in heaven, he didn't want his trouble brought down on Martha Newsom and Caleb.

"Leave the woman be," he hissed, warning in his voice now. "She had nothin' to do with it, I tell you — nor the boy."

Pierce blinked. "We only got the word of a killer for thet," he growled." Sourly, he turned to his crew. "Bring the woman out!"

Three riders dismounted. Ryan could see they were obviously tired, dusty and angry after their long chase. That wouldn't endear them to him.

The hands walked swiftly to Martha stood out front, staring coldly at Pierce. They handled her roughly.

"Damn it, Pierce!" rasped Ryan, feeling impotent and frustrated now. "I told you they is jest innocent people!"

A judge'll decide thet, Tame," Pierce growled. He turned to the crew behind him. "Tie them all up. We'll make camp here for the night — get some real vittles." He glared again at Ryan. "You've led us one hell of a dance, Tame."

He turned back to his men then. "We've had a long ride, an' it'll be an even longer ride back to Fenton." He grinned now. "But there's a big bonus in this for you, boys, I promise."

Rebel yells greeted the announcement. Ryan watched the crew dismount. Rough hands grabbed him then. Nearby Martha Newsom was struggling and kicking now. She wasn't going to go down without a fight. Despite their plight, further admiration warmed Ryan. Martha Newsom was a real gutsy woman. One in a thousand.

He now began to struggle against the hands grabbing him, until a well-placed boot kicked his wound. He cried out harshly as pain seared through him and he dropped to the ground lashing out wildly with his fists, rage thick in his throat. Then he felt ragged pain across his head before he sank into the blackness welling up to him.

★ ★ ★

Ryan fought his way to consciousness through the dull, thobbing pain in his head. The Flying F crew sat around in the night, warming themselves by the two big fires that were licking bright blossoms of orange and yellow light against the velvet, mauve sky; the sickle moon hanging forlornly in it. The homestead outbuildings were gaunt spectres in the background.

Now Ryan could see Pierce, sat outside the cabin on the rocker Ryan had observed by the fireplace in the house. Pierce was wolfing down beans and fatback — his dark, grooved face evil and stone-like in the flickering light.

Ryan focused his gaze on Martha

Newsom now, close by him to his left. She was bound, but she sat impassively staring at the men around the campfires. Caleb was trussed beside her, his young face hollow and pale, but he was working determinedly at the bonds that tied him. The boy had spunk, too, Ryan decided.

He whispered, "You all right, Martha?"

She nodded, her face sallow but calm in the weak, dancing firelight that reached it. In the light her golden hair seemed to glow.

"All right, Ryan," she assured, but her voice could not disguise the strain she was under.

Ryan studied the boy now. "Caleb?"

The boy looked at him, his brown eyes keen. He grinned and nodded. "Okay, Mr Tame."

Ryan was aware now of the dry crusty feeling down the left side of his fire-scarred face. It could only be blood, now dried, from the wound the sixgun that had downed him had made, he decided.

Regret was heavy within him now as he brought his gaze back to Martha. "I'm sorry I've brung you to this, ma'am. Truly sorry."

He was sure a faint smile flickered on Martha's generous mouth for a moment. "Perhaps it would be better if you spent a little less time apologizing for yourself, Ryan. I did what I did willingly." There was, he thought, a gentle, mild rebuke there somewhere.

Ryan didn't feel in a mood to accept it. Damn it, all this was his fault!

He glowered at Pierce, maybe thirty paces away and directed his frustration at him.

"Pierce!" he demanded. "Let these people go! You've no God-damned right to treat them like this!"

"The woman lied for you, Tame," Pierce rasped. "She'll go before the judge!"

"I had a gun on her!" Ryan raged.

"Then she'll be judged on that!" Pierce responded, equally as angry.

Wrath burnt in Ryan's belly. His

impotence, his inability to convince Pierce, seared through him.

"The boy's done nothin'!" he spat. "He was scar't for his mother, was all! At least let him stay — tend their stock."

Pierce stared at him, then at Martha and the boy. For the first time, Ryan thought he saw a glimmer of indecision in Pierce. There were also expectant looks from his crew, too. They appeared to be silently agreeing with Ryan's plea.

Pierce set his lips in a firm, pitiless line and glowered sullenly at the boy, then around the faces of his crew. After fully a minute of taut, brooding silence, Pierce grunted.

"Turn the boy loose in the mornin'," he ordered briskly. "I won't have it said I'm an unfeelin' man."

Ryan was aware now that Pierce's gaze was on him after his decision — almost mocking him. And Ryan realized that, politics-wise, Pierce had scored another telling point at least with his crew. And they were, like it or not, the people that would do the talking in the town. And not in his favour. Accepting that caused anger to sting Ryan.

But Martha Newsom's thankful look for his attempt to get her free compensated for any misgivings he may have had.

Pierce shouted now, to his crew, "We'll sleep until morning. Two men to watch Tame, the boy and the woman. Two hours watch a man. Sunup we head back to Fenton."

His harsh laugh came then. "You know, boys," he observed. "I allus figured Tame's neck sat too close to his shoulders! Guess it won't be long before thet niggle'll be removed."

Raucous howls came from the crew and Martha Newsom's eyes turned like a startled deer's to look at Ryan's cold, glittering stare concentrated solely on the triumphant rancher.

7

BY the time they were riding down the long, brown-green grassy slope into Fenton, Ryan, Martha, Pierce and the Flying F crew showed the effects of the long, dry ride from the Newsom homestead. All were dusty, hot, tired and thirsty.

Long before they got into Fenton — a large, orderly place with low dwellings on the outskirts and a lot of brick-built structures clustered in the centre — folks were coming out to look at the horsemen walking their mounts towards it.

Word, Ryan decided, must have gone on ahead.

Emmet Jones then came riding towards them, big atop his shaggy black stallion. He was a thick-set man with brisk ways. In his round, beefy face were set two chips of stone-grey that passed for eyes. Gripped between his fleshy lips and tobacco-stained, but sound, teeth, was a long, well-chewed, un-lit stogie.

When he saw Ryan the stogie dropped from his lips and the fat-layered eyes narrowed, and disbelief showed clearly on his face. He rubbed his flat nose as though he had either an itch, or was nervous. Ryan realized the sheriff was looking closely at him.

"Ryan Tame?" he queried. "God almighty, what happened to your face, boy? An' dammit, you're supposed to be dead!"

He turned his gaze swiftly to Merton Pierce now, his grey orbs moving half-nervously, half-questioningly to meet the black stare of the rancher. "You've git him trussed, Merton. Why?" His tone was tentative.

"He shot down Oddy Sewell," Pierce informed impatiently. "And I figure he killed Pike Benson, too. An' I'll produce evidence to that end when the time comes."

The rancher's voice grated harshly.

Few words had passed between the group of riders over the last dry miles to Fenton.

"Oddy Sewell?" Jones pursued. "Pike Benson? What you implyin', Merton?" The sheriff looked incredulous.

Emmet Jones now turned his elusive gaze to meet Ryan's blue, cold stare that was keenly watching the by-play.

"What you got to say to that?"

"Nix to both," Ryan gritted. His head was still numb with pain from the blow to it at the Newsom place, and the sun that had beat upon it for two days hadn't helped.

Sheriff Jones turned to Pierce now. "You hear that, Merton?" His eyes came to Martha now and opened wide. "An' who's the lady?"

The rancher's look suddenly turned evil. "Emmet, lissen good," he ground out spitefully, "button thet damned mouth of yours and lock Tame an' the woman up. We'll talk later when I've bathed, eaten an had me half a bottle of good bourbon and a whore

127

at Kate Marsden's. Okay?"

Emmet Jones's eyes narrowed as if he resented Pierce's curt demands. "Better not make it too long a time, Merton," he warned. "Can't hold folks with no evidence against them."

Merton Pierce's stare hardened and his thin, merciless lips tightened. "You'll hold them until I'm good an' ready, Emmet, damn it!" he snapped. "You git my word, ain't you?"

Ryan watched a hint of indignation suddenly invade Emmet Jones's stare. "Sure, sure," he said as if picking his words carefully. "Guess thet's good enough around these parts, for now."

Officiously now, Sheriff Jones eased his horse towards Ryan and Martha. "I'll take them off your hands right now, Merton," he grunted. "Then you and the boys can git straight to your business. But don't be too damned long over it."

Ryan moved restlessly. Damn it, he couldn't sit here and allow Pierce to say what he liked. And the talk of evidence worried him. It had to be false. What evidence could there be? And a Pierce man, or not, Emmet Jones was still the law in this county.

He growled, "He ain't got any evidence at all to say I killed Pike, sheriff. An' I beat Oddy Sewell out of leather fair an' square."

Again the sheriff hesitated then a disbelieving grin spread across his fat face. "You shaded Oddy Sewell?" he ventured incredulously. "Damn it, he's hell out of leather." He added scornfully, "All you is is a dirt farmer."

He guffawed; then uncertainty crossed his features before he soberly turned to Pierce.

"Thet right, Merton?"

Pierce nodded bleakly. "Believe it," he said curtly. "He's damned fast an' a damned killer."

The sheriff rubbed briskly at the stubble on his greasy chin. Then he stared at Ryan and growled, "You bin hidin' your light under a bushel, ain't you, boy?"

Now the sheriff narrowed his stone-grey eyes and turned them back to the rancher. "Well, regarding Pike Benson . . . What would Ryan want to do thet for? They were pals, weren't they?" He looked resentfully at Pierce. "An' I allus found the Tames honest folk, certainly not given to gunplay."

Curiosity stirred in Ryan now at this probing. How much did Emmet Jones know about what had been going on in the valley, he wondered? Here he was witnessing a man that seemed to want the law upheld, yet was careful about challenging Pierce.

Ryan watched Pierce lean forward on his big grey. "You're askin' a lot of questions, Emmet," he growled impatiently. "But I guess that's your job. Tame's been sayin' crazy things like it was me, Benson, Flett an Oddy Sewell who burnt them out at High Mesa."

Ryan felt bound to make the assertion and cut in fiercely, "It was!"

A deadly, evil grin spread across

Pierce's craggy face. "You hear thet, Emmet?" he grunted. "Have you ever heard anything so damned stupid? You know damned well the men he speaks of — includin' me — were in the back room of the Wallace Bar all thet night."

The rancher glared at Ryan. "I figure him seein' his ma burned up like thet an' his own hurts has made him crazy in the head, an' he shot down Pike Benson for what he thought was revenge. Now he's added Oddy Sewell to the list. Thet leaves me an Grant Flett." Pierce turned his attention back to the sheriff. "Emmet, damn it, you can't let a man like thet go runnin' round loose."

Emmet Jones frowned and looked at Ryan and nodded, thoughtfully. "Thet's what Chuck Shannon, the barkeep said: you were in the Wallace Bar, sure enough," he affirmed.

Ryan pounced on that like a dog on raw meat.

"You mean you didn't see them

yourself, sheriff?" he snapped.

The sheriff turned to stare at him resentfully. It seemed to Ryan now, Emmet Jones was getting a little uncomfortable about the way things were unfolding.

"No, I didn't," he said. "I was pounding trail with a posse lookin' for those damned Injuns that caused all the mayhem an' grief we had. I took Chuck Shannon's word on it an' Mr Pierce's an' the boys with him. At the moment five to one odds sounds reasonable to me."

He glared at Pierce now. "Thet still doesn't explain the woman," he said. He hitched uneasily in the saddle. "An' I ain't exactly git facilities for what seems a refined sorta lady."

The twenty-strong Flying F crew were now moving around restlessly on their mounts. One growled, "Dammit, Emmet, you can take what Mr Pierce's sayin' is right . . . Man, we-all have a towerin' thirst here."

Pierce followed the comments up

forcefully. "Emmet, the men an' I have spent near four days in canyon country on this little shindig," he growled. "I git beeves on the range wantin' attention. I have meadows of sweet grass ripe for cuttin'. When the boys have wet their whistles they'll be leavin'. Now, let's have less of this damned hagglin'. You'll git reasons an' your evidence I told you."

Sheriff Jones still looked unconvinced.

Pierce heaved a exasperated sigh then when he saw he still hadn't persuaded the sheriff. "If it'll make you feel better," he went on patiently, "have the woman stay at the Fenton Hotel at my expense. Jest place a guard on her. Thet's the best I can do."

Ryan's gut tightened. Pierce was scoring points again.

Emmet Jones seemed to accept that. "Thet sounds fair enough," he conceded. "You'll stay on to give your evidence fully, Merton?" he requested.

"Jest git Tame behind bars, Emmet," Pierce snorted. "You'll git all the evidence you need."

Merton Pierce sat broodingly looking into his glass of good bourbon in the Wallace Bar. He'd had three large steaks and a pile of vegetables at Ching Liu's place and Gertrude, his favourite girl at Kate Marsden's, had welcomed him warmly and energetically.

Now he gazed through the amber liquid at the closing night outside the bar window. Chuck Shannon charged sky-high for his bourbon and his silence, but it was worth it until his usefulness was expired, then . . .

Pierce grinned. He had decided he had to cultivate a taste for the good things in life now he was climbing the social ladder in the county and beyond. But this Ryan Tame business . . .

He grunted impatiently at his uneasiness. Tame reappearing was a turn of events he didn't want, nor had planned for. Yet good had come out of it. It got rid of the nagging fears that had prodded him ever since the dirt farmer had never been found amongst the ruins and Indian sign they had left at High Mesa. Now he'd get Tame hanged. The woman, Martha Newsom . . . He sucked his lips. Damn it, she was nothing; knew nothing. And who was to say she hadn't been gun-prodded into lying for Ryan Tame? It rang true enough. The woman didn't seem to mean anything to Tame, or him to her. But there was a niggling doubt. He felt sure he knew the woman from somewhere. He shrugged and dismissed the feeling. He'd known many women throughout his life.

And Sheriff Emmet Jones was just a bumbling, weak man, despite his probing and blustering that afternoon. That was why he got him put in the job. He could handle Emmet, he thought comfortingly.

He looked up at Grant Flett sat across the table from him — small, serious, weasel-eyed, sipping whisky. He had three days' black stubble on his narrow, emaciated-looking face.

"Flett," he grunted. "I want you to ride up to the line camp at Pine Ridge. Tell Cat Fetch to come down here. You stay up there until this has blown over."

Flett's amber eyes stared at Pierce briefly, then he tossed off his drink. "Sure, boss."

He rose, went to the bar, ordered a bottle of rotgut and strolled out into the busy main street. He stowed his rotgut, leered a grin at one of the girl's outside Wallace's place then climbed his mustang and rode out into the night.

Pierce grinned sadistically now as the plan that had formed in his mind took its first step. He had enough on Cat Fetch to get the murdering bastard to swear to anything he asked of him.

8

THE following morning Ryan listened to Sheriff Emmet Jones performing his ablutions in the office fronting the stone jailhouse cell he now sat in. There was much coughing and hawking and burbling coming from the sheriff. Then, after quiet minutes and some talk with a woman, the sheriff came in carrying a tray of food and a steaming cup of coffee.

Ryan was grateful to Emmet Jones for having his thigh and head wounds attended to and allowing him to wash thoroughly before the sheriff attended to his own needs the previous afternoon.

Emmet Jones now slid the food he was carrying through the trap made for the job. He said, "Judge Harkness will hold the trial today, Ryan, providin', of course, Merton

Pierce has gathered his evidence."

Ryan attacked the food hungrily and grunted. He fought fiercely to hide the fear that was beginning to creep through him. This was getting too serious. He didn't want to die on the end of a rope, particularly for something he hadn't done. Yet the whole thing seemed to be grinding relentlessly on, placing him ever deeper into trouble and he felt incapable of doing anything about it. The way things were going, Pierce would be grinning up at him as he swung from the gallows in the not too distant future. The thought caused cold fear to course through him and it took an awful lot to control it.

Emmet Jones's stone-grey eyes searched his scarred face. "You got anything thet might help you, son?" he urged. "God, dammit, I jest can't bring myself to believe you shot down Pike Benson. I've known your pa an' you too long. It ain't in you. Not in cold-blood, like it was. Pike had his spine blown apart with a shotgun at close range."

Ryan paused in his eating and hope flowed through him for a few seconds. Walking Antelope would vouch for where he'd been when Pike Benson was shot down! As quickly as it had come, he swamped the thought. If the Hopi did — and Ryan had no doubts that he would — and if things went wrong, Walking Antelope would be the prime target for Pierce's wrath. No, he'd have to fight this one himself.

"I ain't got a damned thing, Emmet," he admitted. "Only my word. Whatever evidence Pierce comes up with concerning me shootin' Pike will be false."

The sheriff heaved a heavy sigh. "Thet's only on your say-so, son," he growled. "I have to be neutral. An' Merton Pierce is a well-respected man hereabouts."

Rage reared in Ryan. He clattered his tin plate down on the small deal table he sat at before staring up at the sheriff.

"He's a murdering killer," he hissed

139

venomously. "Emmet, whether you believe me or not, Pierce put four bullets into me. Oddy Sewell shot down my pa and Sewell, Flett, Benson an' Pierce torched our homestead and barns and burned my ma to death."

Ryan brought his fist, trembling with frustration, down onto the table, bouncing the food on the plate.

Then, feeling as though he was a bull steer butting at stone walls, he slumped his wide shoulders, his irritation simmering in him. "Thet's the damned truth, so help me, Emmet."

Sheriff Jones straightened his bulky figure and paced briskly to and fro before the bars, every now and again his grey eyes flicking to meet Ryan's blue, pleading stare.

"It never has sat right with me," the sheriff admitted worriedly. "It was too damned obvious all the time. An' dammit, there was hardly enough Indians in the mountains to cause such mayhem." His stone-grey gaze came up questioningly. "An' what for? They've been quiet for God knows how long. The evidence we found always pointed too easily to Indians. But, then again, there it was, and the only evidence we had of any substance."

Ryan growled, "It was all staged by Pierce to get his hands on the land throughout the valley."

Emmet Jones rubbed his dark, unshaven chin doubtfully. "He allus paid a fair price," he countered irritably. "Dammit, he paid over the odds to the widows."

"He's a ruthless, clever, scheming bastard," spat Ryan relentlessly. "Allus makin' the kind gesture to cover the killin' an' burnin' an' chiselling thet I learnt, recently, goes way back."

The sheriff still looked doubtful. "Easy to say," he grunted. "An' maybe you're right. There is a mean streak in Pierce. But, without the evidence, son . . . " The sheriff shrugged. "Up to now, Ryan," he added regretfully, "there ain't a damned thing to tie

Pierce into the trouble we had."

"Have you ever leaned on Chuck Shannon at the Wallace Bar?" growled Ryan. "A lot hinges on his say-so that Pierce an' the rest of them were there in the back room the night High Mesa got hit."

Emmet Jones shook his round head. "Hell, why should I have done?" he defended hotly. "Who would remotely connect Pierce, or his boys, with the business? But now . . . Maybe it's time I did have a talk with Chuck."

Ryan stared with new eyes at the sheriff. "I allus figured you to be a Pierce man, bought an' paid for."

Emmet Jones's eyes narrowed and hardened. "Thet's what Pierce thinks, too. But I'm a lawman first, Ryan, a stooge comes a poor second with me. If evidence is brought to convict Merton Pierce you'll soon find which side I'm on."

The sheriff nodded firmly as he turned away. "You'll see," he said over his shoulder, then added, "Understand, son, I've got to play politics to a certain point, but beyond thet . . . "

Ryan watched now as the sheriff moved out up the passageway between the office wall and the cells. Soon he heard the sheriff growl to his deputy, "Mind the shop. I'm going up to the Wallace Bar."

★ ★ ★

Chuck Shannon was a burly, sandy-haired man who grinned at Emmet Jones as the sheriff pushed his thick-set frame through the bat-wing doors of the — at the moment — quiet bar.

"Emmet," the barkeep greeted. "Get you a drink?"

The sheriff shook his head and looked sourly at Shannon.

"Cast your mind back, Chuck," he said grimly. "Back to the night the High Mesa place was burnt out."

Shannon blinked. "Thet's six months ago, Emmet," he grunted uncertainly.

143

He polished a glass avoiding the sheriffs stare. "What you got in mind?"

"Merton Pierce an' his boys Sewell, Flett, Benson," the sheriff growled. "You said they were in the back room playin' poker. Why did you say that? There was no need to. No suspicion was on Merton Pierce."

Chuck Shannon blinked his tawny eyes and licked his thin lips. "God dammit, Emmet, it's months ago now," he grunted. "There was no particular reason as far as I recall. It must have come out in conversation. It was a hot game, I remember."

The sheriff stared stonily at the barkeep. "Ryan Tame has jest tol' me thet Pierce an' the boys were the ones that burned out their place up on High Mesa thet night," he informed. Sheriff Jones narrowed his eyes. "Now, somebody's lyin' to me an' thet ain't nice."

Shannon put down the glass he was polishing. "What are you gettin' at, Emmet?" he snapped. "Tame must be touched out of his mind to say that, like rumour has it. Pierce an' his hands were here the whole night. I swear to God."

The sheriff nodded, looking far from convinced. "Thet's a mighty big man to swear to, Chuck," he said quietly. "Is there anybody else who can back that statement?"

Shannon shuffled down the bar, served a waddy who was gesturing at him irritably. On the way back he picked up a glass and rinsed it in the dish behind the bar and started to polish it. Then he said, "Hell, no, not as I know of," he grunted. "It was a private game. I took their drinks through to them. Most of the men who gather to gawp at big games lit out with the posse when the glow from the fire at High Mesa was seen."

Shannon stared at the sheriff now, his tawny eyes questioning. "You asked Flett, or Pierce?" he demanded. He added sarcastically, "I guess you can't ask Benson an' Sewell . . . From all accounts, it was Tame who ventilated their hides."

At that last remark the sheriff glared uncertainly at the barkeep. But nodded and half-turned to walk away. "I tell you I ain't happy about it, Shannon," he grunted. "You'd better know that, jest in case Ryan Tame proves to be tellin' the truth. Savvy?"

Shannon's face grew long. "Dammit, you've no right to talk thet way, Emmet," he remonstrated.

The sheriff paused at the door, silhouetted in the bright morning sun streaming in through the slats. "I've every damned right, Shannon. Believe it."

★ ★ ★

Pierce belched after his breakfast at Ching Lui's and stared over the rim of his coffee mug at the narrow features of Cat Fetch. Pierce knew Fetch to be a hardcase with a string of robberies with violence behind him. Some he hadn't done time for, but Pierce knew about them as well and was prepared to inform the right authorities, when the time came, if Fetch didn't bend the way the rancher wanted, or, better still, until he could quietly dispose of the owlhoot when his usefulness was at an end.

The hardcase grinned, exposing his yellow teeth through the week-old growth of dark beard on his face. He gulped down the whisky in his hand. He looked to have been in the saddle all night. His trail garb was coated with fine dust.

"An' you want me to say I saw this Tame *hombre* shoot down poor old Pike?" he grunted. He guffawed recklessly then. "Damn' neat, boss," he said smoothly, "considerin' it was me thet done it."

Pierce did not share Fetch's mirth. "Yeah, it is," he said coldly. "You saw it done through the spy-glass I lent you to go up on the ridge with to see if you could pick out any strays in the badlands."

Fetch chortled. "Jeez, what it is to be a thinkin' man," he enthused. "Let me get it straight: I was up on Pine Ridge, like you said, lookin' for strays then, damn me, I saw Ryan Tame shoot down Benson. I reported to you, but you said it couldn't be Tame because he was dead."

Fetch licked his lips and eyed the bottle beside Pierce's right arm. The rancher poured him a small one.

After a noisy swig Fetch said, "How will I know this *hombre*?"

Pierce looked sourly at the owlhoot. "He'll be the one in the dock, numbhead," he growled.

The hardcase's brown, shifty eyes lit up. "Oh, yeah." He grinned sheepishly. "Bin ridin' all night, boss. The brain ain't active jest at the moment."

Pierce glowered at him. "Then git over to the hotel, get yourself a room and git some sleep. I want you clean an' smart an' ready for the trial when it comes up. Savvy?"

Cat Fetch nodded eagerly. "Sure, boss," he said smoothly. "It'll be like fallin' off a log."

Pierce glared with cold, black eyes. "Make sure it is."

★ ★ ★

Ryan said, as Emmet Jones came into the passageway with a plate of hash at noon, "You see Chuck Shannon, Emmet?"

The sheriff pushed the hash through the slot and nodded dourly. "He's stickin' to the story he put out," he said quietly. "He won't budge on it. I've asked around town, too, if there was anybody else could testify different." Ryan met the sheriffs tired looking stare, eager for any crumb that would ease this awful tension now in him.

"Boy," Emmet went on, "there's an awful disinterest in whether or not you're guilty around Fenton. They appear to think Merton Pierce must have some good evidence and they seem satisfied with that. They appear to think your brain really did get scrambled by the ordeal you went through an' some are sorry; but they say it don't give you the right to go around killin' people."

Ryan felt his heart sinking. For the first time, he began to feel resigned to the fact that in the very near future his neck would be stretched.

"Damn it, Emmet," he urged, desperation churning in him. "There must be somebody." He looked at the sheriffs round, glum face. "You seen Grant Flett?"

Emmet Jones shook his head slowly. "He ain't in town," he answered slowly. He met Ryan's blue, pleading stare. 'If you're thinkin' what I think you are thinkin', son Flett ain't goin' to put a rope round his own neck by confessin', now is he?"

Ryan shook his head wearily. "I guess not." Now his eyes turned mean at the thought of Flett. "But he is black guilty," he muttered venomously.

"So is thet rattlesnake-low owner of the Flyin' F." He held the sheriffs sympathetic look. "As God's my judge, Emmet, that's the truth."

Sheriff Jones sighed and held Ryan's stark gaze. "Ryan," he said. "The evidence so far, with regard to the killin's done in the valley, says Pierce is clean. You've admitted killin' Sewell, albeit fair an' square. My gut tells me you're white innocent, but if Pierce comes through with evidence to say you killed Pike Benson . . . "

Jones blinked and looked sadly at Ryan. "Well, son, there isn't a deal I can do."

The sheriff licked his lips and then looked away, as if unable to face Ryan's defeated look. "Your trial is in the courthouse at three o'clock this afternoon," he informed in an official tone and went out.

9

JUDGE HARKNESS was a small, brisk man with short-cropped bristly grey hair and a wasted face. Pince-nez glasses were clasped firmly on his thin, hooked nose. He glowered now with bird-like eyes at the jury sat talking excitedly amongst themselves and rapped his gavel hard on the oak desk he sat at.

"That's enough chattering," he growled. "This is a court of law."

He looked round the full courtroom now, at Merton Pierce sat in one of the chairs at a table on the right of the courtroom, a mean-looking Cat Fetch next to him. Sheriff Jones sat on the left hand side.

The judge stared now at Ryan stood in the dock. "You'll have to speak for yourself, Mr Tame," he advised. "The only lawyer we have is unfortunately out of town. Even so, I am led to believe he would have represented Mr Pierce on the matters before the court in any case."

Judge Harkness stared at the paper in front of him now. "I read the charge against you, Ryan Tame, is the murder of Pike Benson."

The judge's beady eyes came up to meet Ryan's blue stare. "How do you plead?"

Ryan swallowed on the dryness that was now in his throat. "Not guilty, sir."

The judge 'humphed' and swung his gaze to Merton Pierce. "Mr Pierce I believe you have evidence to the contrary? Will you present it, sir?"

Merton Pierce rose, his grooved face set hard and his black eyes glittering. "With pleasure, your honour."

He turned seriously to Cat Fetch, now clean-shaven and with a tidy black broadcloth suit on.

"Take the stand, please, Cat."

Ryan watched the small, narrow-featured, slightly bow-legged hardcase reach the stand and sit down. He was a complete stranger to him.

The clerk came forward. "Do you swear to tell the truth, the whole truth and nothing but the truth, so help you God?" he demanded of Fetch.

Fetch nodded and smiled. "Why, sure."

The judge said, tartly, "Answer correctly!"

Fetch stared evilly for a moment before Pierce's black glare raked him. He grunted, quickly, "I do."

The judge nodded as if satisfied. "Very well. Tell the court in your own words what you saw the day Pike Benson was shot down."

Cat Fetch grinned across at Ryan. Ryan felt his gut go tight. What was going on here? Who was this man? The questions bounced about in his mind, his anxiety rising.

Cat Fetch turned to the jury. "I was asked by Mr Pierce to ride up to Pine Ridge to search out the badlands for strays," he began. "I was to holler down to Pike Benson if I saw any, then, between us, we were to flush them out."

Fetch licked his lips, his brown weasel eyes darting around him. "Well, it was about noon. I spotted mebbe six strays in a washout an' I was ridin' to a position where I could communicate with Pike. It was then I saw him arguin' with this *hombre*." He indicated dramatically to Ryan.

Ryan could contain himself no longer. He snarled, "It's damned lies! Dirty lies!"

The judge glared at him. "Silence! You'll have your say." He turned his sharp stare back to Cat Fetch. "Proceed."

"Well," Fetch started again. "Sudden-like Pike turned away from this *hombre* an' started to ride away." Fetch halted, his voice faltering. Ryan felt his gut knotting tighter.

Then Fetch turned to stare at the judge, his face holding the expression of a man who had witnessed an appalling deed. "Sir, it was awful," he declared. He pointed at Ryan. "That man just upped his shotgun and downed Pike. I had my glass full on him. No one could mistake a face as scarred as thet back-shootin' bastard's — beggin' your pardon, your honour. It was jest a sheer, cold-blooded killin'."

A gasp gushed from the crowd in the court.

His temper now raging in him Ryan made to get out of the dock and cross to the liar on the stand. Emmet Jones's large bulk barred his way, his Colt out and lined firmly up on him.

"Get back, Ryan," he advised softly. "You'd be doin' yourself no good."

Ryan caught the sheriff's sympathetic gaze. "But he's lyin', Emmet," he protested desperately.

Emmet nodded and said quietly, "I think I agree with you, boy, but we ain't a deal goin' for us, have we?"

The gavel was hammering wood again. "Silence! Silence!"

The buzz of talk subsided again.

Then the judge turned to Cat Fetch. "Is that your evidence, sir?"

Fetch nodded emphatically. "Thet's it, judge." He pointed an accusing finger at Ryan, whose blue stare blazed across the courtroom at him. "He killed Pike Benson for sure," Fetch finished, his tone harsh.

The judge waved to him to move in the general direction of Merton Pierce who sat smiling behind the polished prosecuting table. "Then step down."

When Fetch reached Pierce the rancher patted the owlhoot's back as he sat down beside him.

The judge stared at the rancher. "Well, Mr Pierce, have you any more witnesses to put before the court?"

Pierce rose respectfully. "No, sir," he admitted. "Thet's it."

The judge turned to Ryan now and Ryan met the judge's beady stare directly. "What have you to say to the allegations, Mr Tame?"

Ryan held the judge's inquiring gaze. "It's lies, sir."

A patient smile ghosted the judge's lips. "Maybe," he said. "But have you proof that Mr Fetch has come deliberately to this court to lie — on oath, remember — just to get you convicted for this most terrible crime?"

Ryan could not quell the nerves griping in the pit of his stomach. Anger roiled in him. How could this be a court of law? He was innocent! Yet like some lumbering buffalo it was rolling on, the facts presented damning him, though he knew they were lies. They had him black guilty. And he couldn't do a thing about it.

Then the thought suddenly struck him. He clutched at the fleeting straw of hope frantically. He stared at the judge. "I'd like to have Merton Pierce on the stand," he demanded.

The judge frowned before turning to Pierce now glaring at Ryan. Ryan met his stare with ice-blue eyes.

"Take the stand, Mr Pierce, if you please," the judge ordered.

The rancher rose and complied. He

answered the oath, all the time staring into Ryan's scarred, taut face.

The judge said, "Proceed, Mr Tame. Your questions, please."

Ryan licked his lips. "You say Fetch came and told you he saw me shoot down Pike Benson," he probed. "Why didn't you tell Sheriff Jones?"

Pierce narrowed his eyes momentarily. They glittered evilly as they stared at Ryan. Slowly he smiled.

He turned to the judge. "How would it have looked, your honour?" he began. "Tame was presumed dead, taken off by coyotes after that terrible night at High Mesa when the Indians raided. I told Fetch he must have got it wrong, there an' then. Must have."

Pierce hooked his left thumb in his vest pocket. "Jest think, if he'd have come into Fenton an' said that, Fetch would have been branded ten times a fool."

Pierce smiled disarmingly. "I like to feel I look after my hands, your honour. Sort of keep a fatherly eye

159

over them. So I let the matter go." His face became hard then, determined. "I wanted to get after the killer without delay. It's only recent events, which I will now relate, that has proved Fetch right."

Pierce fidgeted now with the fancy black string tie he wore with his grey suit, before catching the judge's bright stare.

"Your honour," he continued, as if reluctantly, "Tame appeared to one of my hands four, five days ago, while he was working on the line camp I'm building at High Mesa. You know I bought the place, judge?"

The judge waved a claw-like hand impatiently. "Yes, yes, Mr Pierce. It's common knowledge in the valley. Go on."

Pierce blinked, a ghost of a smile on his leathery features. "Well, sir, Ryan came with the story that it was myself, Grant Flett, Oddy Sewell and Pike Benson that burned High Mesa and killed the Tame family. He swore to

Jolly Sims, the hand working there, he would kill us all, or see us hanged."

Pierce's look was frank now. "You know, judge," he went on smoothly, "it was proved we were nowhere near High Mesa that night. I've thought a lot about it and the only conclusion I can come to is the injuries Ryan Tame received must have unhinged his mind and turned him against me. It's well-known the Tames' hated my guts. But why he should want to implicate my boys I just don't know . . . "

Pierce shook his head, acting his regret admirably, causing Ryan's anger to burn anew inside him. And his hopes, small as they were, slumped leaving him with a feeling of utter raging impotence and dejection.

Pierce looked appealingly at the judge. "Judge, I know Tame has killed, but maybe he is deranged. I'd be prepared to have him put into care to see if anything can be done for him."

The judge looked with fresh, admiring eyes at the now apparently humble rancher. He smiled.

"Well, sir, that is a most generous offer; a most admirable one," he enthused. "But I'm inclined to view the matter differently. I've dealt with too many murdering ruffians. And, I'm led to believe, Tame has killed Mr Sewell, too. Is that so?"

Pierce nodded. "Yes, sir," he admitted. "But it was a fair shootout."

The judge glared at Pierce reprovingly. "Fair?" he sneered. "Provoked, more like from what I heard. Don't you realize that there is only yourself and Mr Flett left of the men accused by Ryan? To let this man go free, or into care, as you have so magnanimously offered to support, is a folly, sir."

The judge now shook his head vigorously. "No, sir," he said firmly. He turned his stare to Ryan who met his bird-bright gaze with a calm he didn't feel.

Inside Ryan felt numbed, disbelieving that men could lie so smoothly and to such effect. It appalled him. Were all ambitious men like this, he wondered? Surely not.

The judge's thin voice now piped in his ear. "There is only one fate for this man — " he turned to the jury " — death by hanging." Briskly, then, the judge turned his eyes back to Ryan. "What do you say to that?"

Ryan realized the judge was demanding he speak. To apologize, he wondered, or plead insanity, or something? He met the judge's inquiring stare bleakly.

"Seems you've made your mind up, judge," he said quietly. "But I will tell you this: I'm innocent of this crime." He pointed with a scarred finger, his eyes cold blue in his set features, at Merton Pierce. "There's your man. There's the murderer in this valley; either by his own hand or he's had done by his paid killers."

The judge smiled sardonically, yet, for one fleeting moment, Ryan thought there seemed to be a faint hint of doubt there, but . . .

"You have produced no evidence,

only innuendo," the judge went on precisely. "That is no good in a court of law. We have heard the testimony of an eyewitness to say, emphatically, that you killed Pike Benson. It leaves the jury only one verdict."

The judge turned to the twelve men. "Well, what's it to be? Do you want to retire to consider?"

The foreman stood. Ryan knew him to be Wilfred Green, the owner of the general store. Green looked half-apologetically at him.

"From what's been said, guess Ryan's as guilty as hell," he muttered and sat down.

Again the buzz of talk rose in the courtroom, but it was subdued, as if a trifle unsure.

The judge's waspish look claimed Ryan's. "Well, I guess that's it," he said briskly. "You anything further to say before sentence is passed?"

Cold, hard disbelief had set within Ryan. "Sure," he said. "The woman, Martha Newsom, who was accused of being my accomplice, is innocent. I held a gun on her to lie for me. I ask you to let her go, judge."

"Sheriff Jones?" The judge's eye fastened on the burly frame of the sheriff sat quietly. "What's this?"

"Merton Pierce brought the charge, your honour," Emmet grunted. The sheriffs grey look, when he turned it to the rancher, was cold and hard. He related briefly Martha's part in Ryan's capture. Then he said, "You see fit to drop it, Pierce?"

Merton Pierce's face devoid of emotion, then it switched to a look of conciliation. "It's a black enough day, judge," he grunted. "I guess what Tame says about the business has the ring of truth."

The judge turned to Sheriff Jones. "Release the woman, Emmet. Give her the court's apologies."

He turned his beady gaze to Ryan now. "And you, Tame, will be taken out at noon tomorrow and hanged until you are dead in the town square."

10

RYAN became aware of a tap on the outside bars of the cell first, then the voice of Caleb Newsom.

"Mr Tame?" It came as a tense whisper.

Ryan raised himself cautiously from the pine board bench that served as a bed. Then, wincing at the pain in his leg, he went to the bars.

He climbed onto the small table below the grill that had a washbasin on it.

He peered through the bars into the dark alley behind the jailhouse. Sure enough, the taut face of Caleb showed in the pale light of the quarter moon. The boy sat astride a sturdy farm horse. Then Ryan saw the gun being poked towards him, clasped in the boy's hand. For a moment, disbelief at this turn in his fortunes surged through Ryan. He soon overcame it.

Without speaking he grasped the Colt eagerly.

"Best I can do, Mr Tame," the boy continued. "It's loaded. Ma was goin' to bring it, but I figured it wasn't woman's work."

A warmth of feeling flooded through Ryan. The deep despair he had wallowed in, since being brought back from the courthouse, dispersed.

"More than enough, boy," he grunted softly, gratefully. "Now git. You an' your'n have helped me more than enough with my troubles."

The boy nodded. "Luck, Mr Tame," he said quietly, and melted back into the night.

Quickly now, Ryan checked the revolver. It was loaded and in good order.

He licked his lips. Now to lure Emmet into the back, which wouldn't be difficult, he reckoned.

"Emmet? You there?"

His voice rang startlingly, breaking the quiet surrounding the jailhouse.

Ryan heard a grunt, then the sound of a chair scraping back over boards.

"Somethin' you want, Ryan?" The sheriffs voice was unmistakable.

"Could do with a drink, if it ain't too much trouble, Emmet."

Ryan heard the sheriff grunt again. "Git some coffee simmerin'," he said. "How does thet sound?"

"Better an' better, Emmet," Ryan answered, his gut beginning to tighten slowly.

Ryan could hear the sheriff moving about the office now — hear the clank of a tin cup, the sound of fluid being poured, then the clump of boots making for the cells.

Emmet appeared in the passageway carrying a mug of steaming coffee. He came close to the bars and pushed the cup through.

"Here you are, boy," he grunted. "Pipin' hot."

With the speed of a striking snake,

Ryan clamped his iron grip on the sheriffs wrist and poked the gun through the bars, holding the barrel close under Emmet's red, bulbous nose. The coffee mug clattered to the ground, its brown contents spreading across the cell floor.

"You know I don't want to kill you, Emmet," he hissed. His voice hardened. "But if I have to . . . "

The sheriff looked at the gun for a moment with startled grey eyes, then a slow grin spread across his features.

"I don't know how you done it, Ryan," he said, "an' I ain't askin'. Son, you jest tie me up an' lock the cell. Don't forget to gag me, too."

Ryan smothered his momentary astonishment with prompt elation. "Then get to opening the cell, Emmet," he urged.

Within two minutes Emmet was saying, as Ryan tied him up after he had relieved him of his sixgun, "Go after Grant Flett and Cat Fetch, Ryan," he advised, wincing as Ryan tightened the bonds. "If you have to beat a damned confession out of them. Though I didn't tell you to do thet," he cautioned.

"Know where they are?" Ryan probed.

The sheriff grunted, wriggling to find a more comfortable position within the bonds now holding him. "Ching Lui said Pierce had sent Flett up to the Pine Ridge line camp," he offered eagerly. "Fact is, I was goin' to ride up there myself tonight see what I could get out of him. An' I know for sure Cat Fetch is playin' cards in the Valley Bar."

Ryan said then, gratefully, "I owe you, Emmet . . . "

The sheriff scowled. "I jest hope to God my instincts about you are right, boy."

Smiling at that Ryan began to unship the soiled bandana from around his neck. "Sorry about this, Emmet," he grunted, "but it's the only gag I've got to hand."

The sheriff grimaced and stared

aghast. "God, I ain't standin' for thet," he protested. He nodded downwards frantically. "Use the clean handkerchief Mrs Jones tucked in my vest pocket before I came out."

Ryan swiftly found the large, plain white square of linen and applied it to Emmet's mouth. Then, at the cell door, he looked back with steady eyes.

"I'll be back," he said.

The sheriffs stone-grey eyes glowered over his gag. All he could offer was an impatient, muffled grunt.

Ryan moved cautiously to the doorway now, leading into the office. The room was deserted. His swift glance found a bench against the street window, two chairs drawn up to a small table to his right, a big desk with papers strewn over its top and several drawers down each side of it. And behind the desk, the gun-rack.

Ryan found his rig, the Colt stuck in the holster, cartridges in the belt. With the rifles in the rack, his Winchester.

Swiftly he buckled on the familiar

rig and adjusted it into the position most favoured for his fast draw and tied it down. Grim, but with a warm satisfaction flooding through him now he moved, limping, towards the door.

The broad street leading away from the jailhouse was almost deserted. Just the odd waddy reeled from one bar to the next. The occasional rouged floozy leaned against clapboards taking the cool night air.

Ryan slid out through the door and melted into a dark shadow near the alley running down the side of the jailhouse. First, he had to get a horse. Strawberry, as Caleb had named her, preferably.

He knew, when Pierce was in town, the rancher used the livery barn to the north end of Fenton, in preference to the one east. It remained for Ryan now to bluff his way past the hostler there and an idea came quickly to mind that might just help him do that . . .

At the dark maw of the livery barn he paused. He could see a faint light inside. Quickly now, he wrapped his bandana around his face, shading his features as much as possible — replaced his stetson, and walked in.

The old ranny stared up at him, then grinned. "Yer git tooth trouble," he said triumphantly.

Ryan was surprised. It was better than he expected. He groaned for effect. "It ain't damned funny, old timer."

He moaned again. "I've come for the strawberry roan belongin' to Mr Pierce," he mumbled. "Gotta take it back to the Flyin' F. Some gunslinger named Tame supposed to have stolen it."

The hostler grinned in the dull yellow light coming from the smelling, untrimmed lamp. "Tomorrow, thet galoot is goin' to provide the best entertainment this town has had in many a long day," crowed the hostler, his grin exposing broken, rotted teeth.

Ryan grunted and moaned again, holding his jaw hidden underneath the bandana, keeping into the shade as much as possible. "An' I'll miss it," he growled. "Gotta get back to the Flyin' F."

The hostler 'he-hawed'. "Some folks jest ain't born lucky," he chortled. "I'll git the horse."

"The saddle, too," Ryan added quickly. "Pierce figures, due to all the trouble Tame has put him to, some hand on the spread should have the use of it. Fact is, he's given it to me. I got to ride the roan back."

The hostler grunted. "'Tain't nothin'," he scoffed. "Jest a pile of worn leather, needin' stitchin'. You're welcome."

The hostler turned suspiciously now, his eyes narrowing, and Ryan's gut tightened. "Say," he growled. "I saw the Flyin' F hands ridin' out earlier this evenin', grumpy as ass-kicked bears at not bein' able to stop fer the hangin'. Why weren't you with them?"

"Mr Pierce held me back on a job here." Ryan licked his lips, shrugged. "He pays the wages. I don't ask."

The hostler nodded as if satisfied

with the explanation. "Yup. Guess thet's so."

Ryan groaned again and held his jaw. "Damn the tooth."

The hostler hooted again. "Here, I'll throw the saddle on the mare fer you," he offered, as if now sorry for Ryan's feigned plight.

Ten minutes later Ryan thanked the hostler and climbed up and eased the roan into the night, feeling comforted with the smooth, silken motion of the animal's muscles under him.

He kept to the alleys behind the main drag. His eyes soon got used to the weak light of the quarter moon, but it was strong enough for him to pick out features some distance away.

At the rear of the Valley Bar he dismounted. Quickly now he moved up the alley to the front of the sleazy drinking den. His cautious stare through the dirty street window found Cat Fetch dealing cards, his narrow features, under his low-crowned black stetson, swarthy in the yellow light.

Ryan's eyes narrowed. He had to get Fetch out of there. He searched his mind for more answers. Fire seemed favourite. It would be no big loss to the town, the Valley Bar anyway. But, he figured, it needn't come to that. Just enough fire to cause a little mayhem, a little panic.

He studied the street. It was deserted. The time was after midnight. Grim-faced now he unhitched the street lamp hanging from the awning over the haberdasher's.

Almost nonchalantly he tossed it in through the open door and waited. Bright flame soon followed the tinkle of glass. For moments there was a pregnant silence before strings of curses came and men began erupting out of the bat-wing doors calling for buckets and water. Ryan mingled with them. He closed in on Fetch, who was racing for the fire-bucket outside the butcher's.

Roughly, his anger hot within him for this lying bastard, Ryan got the owlhoot by the scruff of his neck and slammed him down the dark alley next to the butcher's and rammed his gun into the thin hardcase's side.

"Where's your horse?" he rasped. As he spoke he unshipped the owlhoot's hardware and threw it into the night.

Cat Fetch's weasel eyes came up to look into Ryan's blazing blue gaze. Fear clear in the owlhoot's stare he pointed at a poor-looking buckskin stood hipshot at the Valley Bar tie-rail.

Fiercely, Ryan shoved him forward, boring the Colt barrel into the hardcase's back. "Git it," he ground out. "Lead it down the alley. One bad move and I'll blow your spine apart. I got nothin' to lose."

Ryan walked with the owlhoot, gritting his teeth against the pain in his thigh, into the confusion of men now running back and forth with buckets splashing water from the horse trough nearby. Fetch un-hitched the buckskin and, responding to an angry prod from Ryan, moved with it back into the alley.

Reaching his own roan Ryan prodded Fetch again and grabbed the reins of the buckskin.

"Climb up!" he demanded.

White with fright now, Cat Fetch swung up into the buckskin's saddle and sat staring dumbfounded at Ryan. "What you for, Tame?" he quavered.

"You'll find out you lyin' bastard!" Ryan grated.

Still gripping the reins, Ryan swung up onto the roan and, tugging the reins of Fetch's buckskin, melted into the blue-purple night heading towards Pine Ridge.

★ ★ ★

Pale dawn was streaking the eastern sky.

Ryan looked down on the one-roomed line camp tucked into a fold in the ground on the south slope of the humpback that was Pine Ridge. Cat Fetch now lay behind him, trussed up tight, a gag stuck in his gash-like mouth. Close by, the horses cropped grass on short ropes.

The hut was very quiet. No blue smoke wreathed out of the stone stack. A hobbled black stallion cropped grass in a loosely-roped remuda.

Licking his lips Ryan unshipped his Colt and hobbled down the slope behind the cabin. He came softly against the peeling pine wall and listened. Nothing.

He worked his way round the front now. The glassless window was shuttered. Swallowing on his dry throat, his senses tuned to the slightest thing that would spell trouble, Ryan worked his way to the door, the pain in his thigh reminding him he couldn't kick it in. With infinite care, he unhitched the latch before slamming it open.

Flett's amber eyes were opening, bleary and round with fright, as Ryan crashed in. The waddy's narrow face froze with disbelief. His hand clawed towards the gun hung on the bed-post by his head. Ryan's slug had Flett shouting his alarm as it smashed into the wall inches from him showering him with yellow splinters.

"Not wise," suggested Ryan. A thin smile now played on his lips.

Flett trembled visibly now. "Oh, my God, Ryan Tame!"

"Ain't it the truth."

Ryan's pitiless blue stare found the waddy's frightened gaze. "You got a whole lot of talking to do, you murderin' bastard."

Flett sat up in bed now his alarm complete. "What — what you goin' to do?" he whined.

"You're goin' back to Fenton, Flett," Ryan informed. "You're goin' to sing like a canary."

"Weren't only me!" protested the frightened waddy. "You know thet! Pierce paid us big bonuses!"

"Sure I know," Ryan hissed. He wanted, there and then, to blast this pathetic rat to hell. But . . . He glared at the puncher. "Jest sing it all to Sheriff Jones an' the judge. Maybe, if you sing loud enough, you'll perhaps get off with a ten year stretch."

Hope glimmered into Flett's amber stare. "You figure?"

Ryan grinned mirthlessly. "Hell, why not, Flett? You an' Fetch together should be able to make a mighty convincing song."

"Cat Fetch?" demanded Flett, still a little bemused by his rude awakening. "Where does he fit in?" Flett's eyes became knowing. "Oh, yeah, he was in on the burning of Barton's place down near Clear Creek."

Quiet elation crept into Ryan. Seems this canary was going to sing his heart out. "Thet's interesting, Flett. Damn me, everybody thought it was Indians!"

Flett narrowed his amber stare. He seemed to be calming now that his life appeared not to be in imminent danger.

"You know different to thet, Tame," he growled.

At so swift and nonchalant a dismissal of his parents' fate, swift anger raked

Ryan like a naked spur. The horrendous picture of his mother's burning body claimed his mind's eye again causing mad rage to invade his thinking.

He crossed the cabin floor and grabbed Flett by his grimy longjohns and hoisted him to his feet. He crashed his fist into the alarmed face of the waddy. Flett screamed his pain as blood poured from his mashed nose and the fear came back to his eyes as he crashed to the dirt floor.

Then Ryan put a rein on his murderous feelings. He fought to calm himself, his body quivering.

Finally in control of his seething emotions he scowled at the cowering puncher. "Get dressed you damned scum!" he ordered.

Flett complied with alacrity, all the time his scared eyes watching Ryan, who stood glaring him, his Colt lined menacingly on him.

The sun's rays were warming them by the time — horse saddled and Flett aboard it, his arms trussed to his sides — Ryan hobbled back up the hill behind the waddy, his Colt trained on the owlhoot's back. Ryan fought down the desire to ram lead into the body of the murdering puncher.

No, he had to get these two to the sheriff and the judge and hope to God they'd tell all they knew.

11

IT was two am. Ryan was grimly riding to Pine Ridge.

Merton Pierce was savouring his bourbon nightcap in the Wallace Bar. His straw boss, Hiram Banes, ducked in through the batwings and sat at his table and stared at him with watery blue eyes, his jaw working on a chaw.

"Tame's got Cat Fetch," he mouthed and spat into a nearby cuspidor.

Pierce's black eyes stared disbelievingly at the foreman. "What the hell you talkin' about, Banes?" he growled. "Tame's in jail."

"No, he ain't," contradicted the straw boss. "Utah Fagan saw him take Fetch during the confusion the fire caused up at the Valley Bar."

Pierce's eyes were now filled with rage as well as disbelief. "Then why didn't Utah deal with it?" he demanded.

"Pie-eyed drunk, boss," muttered Banes. "Couldn't stand."

Pierce muttered black curses under his breath, his glittering, rage-filled eyes staring at his tall, gangling straw boss. He had five men he trusted — Banes, Utah Fagan, Harley Simmons, Sewell and Flett. Only Banes, Simmons and Utah were now with him and Utah was drunk. The bastard would have to sober up quick. But there was another possibility.

"Then how the hell can you be sure Tame took Fetch if Utah's the way he is?" he grated.

Banes blinked. "Checked," he said briefly. "Guess we ought to go up to the jailhouse, see what's happened up there."

Pierce got up swiftly, his rangy body lithe and taut, belying his late middle-age.

"Damned right," he grunted. "Emmet has some explainin' to do."

Then he stopped mid-stride in the middle of the dimly-lit bar, his long-fingered sinewy right hand coming to his mouth. "On second thoughts, Banes . . . "

He brought his black stare up to meet the straw boss's watery look. "Get Simmons an' sober up Utah. We'll be ridin'."

His stare still held the straw boss. "You know, I'm gittin' not to have a deal of faith in how Emmet will jump," Pierce said. "He came down too easy on Tame's side yesterday. We'll deal with this one ourselves. I figure Fetch has crowed and Tame is headin' out to the Pine Ridge line camp to work on Flett. Meet me here in half an hour."

Banes nodded and moved out into the night.

Pierce stood thinking hard for fully ten minutes outside the Wallace Bar — watched a dog sniff around one of the awning posts fronting the barber's in the pale moonlight before cocking a leg. That hound had no business being out, he thought sourly, interrupting his more serious thoughts.

Then the plan he was wrestling with

gelled, with all the detail he was used to.

Warmth filling him he walked quickly up to the sheriffs office and jailhouse. He could see a light inside shining yellow, pale light onto the desolate street outside. He approached the window cautiously and peered in. The office was deserted. Nobody at the desk, or table.

He tried the door. It was open and he glided inside. As a precaution, he pulled out his longbarrelled Colt. He tip-toed across the room to the door leading to the rear and the jailhouse. He took a narrow-eyed perusal of the cells. Then grim humour filled him to see Emmet Jones slumped, trussed like a chicken in the nearest cell, his head dropped, his eyes closed, snoring.

Pierce backed out into the light of the office again. Emmet could stay there. He didn't want the law blundering about while he executed the plan now clear-cut in his mind. He'd have to assume Emmet had elected to work the night shift and his deputies were home until six o'clock the coming morning. If he figured right, he could lay all his ghosts to rest this day and he could start and work hard towards getting the governorship of the state. It wasn't beyond a man of his ambition, he figured.

Though Tame was the prime target, he thought grimly, Flett and Fetch had become expendable, too.

He extinguished the lamp and walked into the cool night.

★ ★ ★

Ryan came out of the trees and settled down to move dust across the brown-green undulating lands stretching towards Fenton, strewn haphazardly with huge clumps of boulders. He figured by mid-afternoon he would be presenting himself to Emmet Jones and the judge and Cat Fetch and Grant Flett would be singing.

Flett and Fetch jogged on their

horses before him, heads down, sullen and morose. The sun was a blazing white orb above them now, mercilessly beating down. Flying F beeves were already under the shelter of the brush and cottonwoods around them, but he figured he wouldn't encounter any riders this end of the range. It was country, he figured, you entered only to round up mavericks, or beeves for the trail to Kansas.

It was the sudden stopping of his horse and its ears pricking up and its quick short whinney that set him on edge, his blue gaze searching the range before him. Broken ground rocky, studded with scrub oak and brush.

There were a dozen possible places for ambush up there, he knew. But why should there be? At worst it could perhaps be Emmet Jones with a posse, if it was anything.

Flett and Fetch also seemed to become aware that a change had subtly taken place in the atmosphere of the morning, that a tension had come to it, a breathless expectancy.

The crisp crack of a rifle dispelled any further uncertainty. Flett gave a cry and catapulted off his mount driven by the force of the lead that hit him to lie gasping and moaning in the dust of the trail.

Tame kicked his strawberry roan forward and grabbed the reins of Fetch's horse. More shots were ringing out now and lead was singing through the air, too close for comfort.

Soon Ryan was kicking for the cover of a rash of large boulders maybe a hundred yards off trail, towing Fetch's protesting mare behind him.

Flett's boney black turned and trotted after them neighing shrilly, the stirrups flapping wildly at its flanks. Flett was on his hands and knees crawling behind it. Another shot rang out and Flett dropped forward with a harsh cry and became still.

Ryan thundered into the shelter of the rocks and dropped out of the saddle, pulling out his Winchester as he went. He ran towards Cat Fetch now and hauled him roughly out of the saddle and shoved him, unprotesting, towards the rocks.

Ryan's voice grated as he said, "Guess whoever's up there ain't a friend of yours, or mine. Git your head down, Fetch."

Fetch's brown, scared eyes found Ryan's. "Cut me loose, Tame," he demanded. "Give me a gun."

Ryan gave him a sardonic grin. "Go to hell, Fetch," he growled. "Keep your head down, is all."

He crawled forward then and gingerly lifted his stetson from his head. Perched on the end of his Winchester he held it up. Four shots crashed out and the hat spun away to rest on the dust yards away.

Ryan rolled over twice to his left and came up and peered through a gap in the rocks to see a figure moving in the rocks some hundred yards away. He took swift, but calm aim and squeezed off and was satisfied to hear a sharp cry jar across the ground between them.

A long silence ensued after that, then the shout came. "Tame. Come out. You're goin' back to hang."

Surprise flooded through Ryan to begin with. No doubting Merton Pierce's voice. Then his surprise dispersed. No way was Pierce going to allow him to walk away from here. It was a heaven-sent chance for the killer to get rid of him for once and all.

"You gettin' to killin' your own men now, Pierce?" Ryan shouted, "Thet's Grant Flett you just shot down."

"He must have got in the way of the bullet for you," came back the mocking reply. "Too bad."

Ryan snorted his contempt for the murdering devil before him. "Once, maybe, but twice?" he grated. "I figure it different. He knows too much, like Fetch here an' maybe one or two more. And this is as good a place as any to get rid of him. How many more are in line for the treatment before you're clean, Pierce?"

The rancher snorted. "You're crazy."

"I doubt if Flett thinks so now," Ryan countered smoothly. He looked sideways at Fetch cowering in a niche in the rocks nearby. "How about you, Fetch?"

A barrage of shots came after that and lead spanged and hummed angrily through the rocks.

Ryan licked his lips and crouched under the cover of the rock he was behind. And he knew he was in a bad position here. He had to get Pierce to act reckless, start exposing himself.

"Pierce?" he shouted. "Emmet Jones'll more than likely be ridin' this trail shortly with a posse of worthy citizens. What will you tell him about Flett an' Fetch, an' maybe me?"

"You resisted arrest, Tame." Pierce sounded smug and confident.

"But what if we're still alive when he arrives?" Ryan suggested. "I'm sure Fetch here will want to give up along with myself an' maybe sing a little, too."

There was a silence for a few moments. Then the harsh reply battered its way through the intervening rocks.

"Don't bank on it," Pierce barked.

For a brief moment Ryan bobbed up to see the tall straw boss of the Flying F, Hiram Banes, running long-legged to the right. With a slight pang of desperation Ryan released two hot hunks of lead towards the straw-boss, accompanied by the crash of his Winchester, before ducking back as a barrage of shots savaged the rocks around him, sharding dark rock splinters in all directions.

Pretty soon, now he'd given Pierce the picture, all hell was going to be let loose, Ryan thought it desperately.

He rolled into a better position, then crawled snake-low to his right past Fetch, who implored,

"Cut me loose, Tame. We're in this together, dammit."

Ryan ignored him, bellying through the rocks to come up scanning the rough ground on his right flank.

194

Banes was running towards the rocks now, crouched low. To Ryan's left, another barrage of shots sounded. Ryan ducked instinctively, but the bullets were whining harmlessly away from him and a grim satisfaction filled him. For the moment he knew they had lost him.

Banes was bearing down on the rocks he was in now. The straw-boss's face showed his tension. His teeth were bared, the lines of his long face stretched taut. Ryan pulled off, two harsh shots that thwacked snarling sound into the hills around. And Banes's face was melting into a bloody mess — tissue and bones spraying out of the back of his head, his brown derby going with them.

The straw-boss continued his headlong rush for a couple of moments before he collapsed into a tangled heap, only his legs threshing.

The shooting from Pierce's position rose to a crescendo in answer.

Ryan was already crawling back,

bellying across the dry, rocky ground to find a fresh position.

Fetch was sobbing now, rolling and then working himself crab-like to a more secure niche.

"You're a bastard, Tame," he was bawling. "A bastard! Cut me loose!"

Then Ryan was aware that a man was diving into the rocks to his left and he lashed two shots at him before high-tailing back towards the rocks at his rear, ignoring the pain of his wounded thigh, and penetrated their cover thankfully.

Fetch was on his feet now and hobbling after him, hindered by the ropes securing his arms, and still cursing. Two shots rang out and Fetch shouted with pain. Ryan could already see blood blossoming from the owlhoot's shoulder.

"Damn it," Fetch was screaming. "It's me, Mr Pierce! May your rotten, stinkin' hide burn in hell!"

Fetch collapsed into a heap near Ryan and crabbed for cover between two slabs of rock sobbing with pain.

"Know your friends, Fetch," Ryan growled harshly.

Ryan saw murder in the owlhoot's dark, swarthy features as he stared back at him. Fetch glowered, his brown eyes evil. "I'll see thet bastard hangs now!" he grated.

Ryan grinned despite his bad position. "Amen to thet, Fetch," he growled.

Then Fetch's eyes rounded as they looked past Ryan, over his shoulder. "Behind you, Tame!"

Like a coiled spring, Ryan released his muscles, sending himself catapulting to his right, pulling his Colt as he did so.

Through the dust he could see Utah Fagan stood up, rifle aimed at him.

With the speed and accuracy instilled in him by Macey Fenner over long months, Ryan drove two shots towards the barrel-chest of the Flying F waddy.

Thrown by Fetch's shout and Ryan's sudden move, Fagan's first shot went wild, his second kicked dust an inch from Ryan's ear. But that was all. He dropped, stone-dead, as two of Ryan's .45 slugs embedded in his heart.

Breathless silence descended now. The sun, Ryan realized, was a burning orb above them, sucking them dry.

Maybe fully a minute passed before Pierce's uncertain voice called, "Utah?"

"He's dead, Pierce," Ryan crowed. "You're fast runnin' out of men and time. Fetch here says he wants to see you hang."

Then the sound of horse's hoofs came, pounding the hard earth behind the rocks Pierce was holed up in.

Then Pierce's desperate call came, "Come back, Simmons, you cowardly, no-good sidewinder. Damn you — come back!"

Ryan couldn't prevent his elation bursting through as a laugh. "Are the rats deserting the ship, Pierce?" he demanded.

With that, Ryan stood up. He figured that Pierce was the last of the scum; that there was only the rancher left in the rocks. If there had been more, Simmons would not have run out on Pierce like he had, he reasoned. He was guessing, but he figured it was a good guess.

Now, by God, he wanted Pierce alive.

He began to run — a looping run, keeping to the cover of the rocks; all the time closing in on the clump he knew Pierce was holed up in. He had to gamble Pierce would not be expecting the move — that he would maybe think a dirt farmer was not capable of such blatant aggression. Before the death of his parents, he maybe wouldn't have been, he thought grimly. But now . . . his need for vengeance returned, burning into his soul.

He came upon the horse first, secured to a limb of mesquite, swatting flies with a chestnut-coloured tail.

He hunkered down now, and crept forward with cougar-like caution. His nerves tautened in his gut. He could feel his body trembling slightly with the heightened awareness of danger that was filling him.

Then he heard the noise of a stone being dislodged above him and to his left. It sounded as though somebody was moving around up there anxiously. And it had to be Pierce.

Ryan began to move up slowly, pausing often to listen and wait before moving again.

Then he saw Pierce, his rangy back to him, his hair black and limp with sweat under his brown stetson. He was peering forward anxiously, his Winchester held firmly in his hands.

Ryan said, "If you don't drop it, Pierce, I'll shoot you. You've got the choice. A choice ma an' pa never had."

Pierce tensed; his long, bony fingers whitened on the steel and wood of his rifle. For long moments he stood there trembling, his head half-turned, his body rigid, then he dropped the gun as though it was red hot metal and cursed.

12

RYAN was boiling coffee when he saw the riders approaching. Sure enough, he could see Emmet Jones's burly frame filling the saddle on a big buckskin stallion. A posse was strung out behind him.

Behind Ryan, Pierce lay tied and cursing. Fetch was propped against a rock, weak from blood loss. Ryan had patched him up as best he could. But the real bonus was Flett was still alive. A jagged wound under his arm and a nasty crease in his skull — and raging anxious to put Pierce on the gallows.

"You're late, Emmet," Ryan grunted as he poured coffee and offered the red-faced, sweating sheriff a full cup. "I got me two birds just longin' to sing an' another prime for the gallows."

Emmet Jones nodded and accepted the coffee gratefully. "There's a little lady back in Fenton mighty worried about you Ryan, an' a boy who thinks you're the next best thing to Thanksgivin'."

Ryan brought his blue gaze up quickly. "Martha Newsom?" he said tentatively.

The sheriff nodded, a smile twitching his thick lips. "Huh, huh. If you want to be ridin' on, boy," he offered. "I'll see to things here. She sure seemed keen on thankin' you fer speakin' up on her behalf yesterday in court."

Ryan studied the florid sheriff. "Thet the truth?"

Emmet's stone-grey eyes came up twinkling. "The whole." He smiled.

Ryan jerked straight with a speed that obviously startled Emmet Jones. He crossed to his roan — his thigh wound forgotten — stood hip-shot against the mesquite it was tied to. Once in the saddle, Ryan stared down at the sheriff hunkered by the coffee pot.

"I'd be obliged if you'd collect my

gear an' bring it in with you, Emmet," he said.

"Only if I git an invite to the weddin'," grinned the sheriff, his eyebrows raised expectantly.

Ryan could not prevent his face reddening.

"Damn me," he blurted. He smiled. "It's too early fer that. But a real nice thought though."

And he rode off planning how best to get a beautiful widow to marry a scarred and ugly sheep farmer who was unclipping his gunbelt and pushing it into his saddlebags, mindful of an old gunfighter's request that he should once the job was done.

And he grinned and started to whistle, despite the searing heat of the afternoon sun, and urged Strawberry into a gallop.

FIGHTING RAMROD
Charles N. Heckelmann

Most men would have cut their losses, but Frazer counted the bullets in his guns and said he'd soak the range in blood before he'd give up another inch of what was his.

LONE GUN
Eric Allen

Smoke Blackbird had been away too long. The Lequires had seized the Blackbird farm, forcing the Indians and settlers off, and no one seemed willing to fight! He had to fight alone.

THE THIRD RIDER
Barry Cord

Mel Rawlins wasn't going to let anything stand in his way. His father was murdered, his two brothers gone. Now Mel rode for vengeance.

ARIZONA DRIFTERS
W. C. Tuttle

When drifting Dutton and Lonnie Steelman decide to become partners they find that they have a common enemy in the formidable Thurston brothers.

TOMBSTONE
Matt Braun

Wells Fargo paid Luke Starbuck to outgun the silver-thieving stagecoach gang at Tombstone. Before long Luke can see the only thing bearing fruit in this eldorado will be the gallows tree.

HIGH BORDER RIDERS
Lee Floren

Buckshot McKee and Tortilla Joe cut the trail of a border tough who was running Mexican beef into Texas. They stopped the smuggler in his tracks.

BRETT RANDALL, GAMBLER
E. B. Mann

Larry Day had the choice of running away from the law or of assuming a dead man's place. No matter what he decided he was bound to end up dead.

THE GUNSHARP
William R. Cox

The Eggerleys weren't very smart. They trained their sights on Will Carney and Arizona's biggest blood bath began.

THE DEPUTY OF SAN RIANO
Lawrence A. Keating and
Al. P. Nelson

When a man fell dead from his horse, Ed Grant was spotted riding away from the scene. The deputy sheriff rode out after him and came up against everything from gunfire to dynamite.

FARGO: MASSACRE RIVER
John Benteen

The ambushers up ahead had now blocked the road. Fargo's convoy was a jumble, a perfect target for the insurgents' weapons!

SUNDANCE: DEATH IN THE LAVA
John Benteen

The Modoc's captured the wagon train and its cargo of gold. But now the halfbreed they called Sundance was going after it . . .

HARSH RECKONING
Phil Ketchum

Five years of keeping himself alive in a brutal prison had made Brand tough and careless about who he gunned down . . .

FARGO: PANAMA GOLD
John Benteen

With foreign money behind him, Buckner was going to destroy the Panama Canal before it could be completed. Fargo's job was to stop Buckner.

FARGO:
THE SHARPSHOOTERS
John Benteen

The Canfield clan, thirty strong were raising hell in Texas. Fargo was tough enough to hold his own against the whole clan.

PISTOL LAW
Paul Evan Lehman

Lance Jones came back to Mustang for just one thing — revenge! Revenge on the people who had him thrown in jail.

HELL RIDERS
Steve Mensing

Wade Walker's kid brother, Duane, was locked up in the Silver City jail facing a rope at dawn. Wade was a ruthless outlaw, but he was smart, and he had vowed to have his brother out of jail before morning!

DESERT OF THE DAMNED
Nelson Nye

The law was after him for the murder of a marshal — a murder he didn't commit. Breen was after him for revenge — and Breen wouldn't stop at anything . . . blackmail, a frameup . . . or murder.

DAY OF THE COMANCHEROS
Steven C. Lawrence

Their very name struck terror into men's hearts — the Comancheros, a savage army of cutthroats who swept across Texas, leaving behind a bloodstained trail of robbery and murder.

SUNDANCE: SILENT ENEMY
John Benteen

A lone crazed Cheyenne was on a personal war path. They needed to pit one man against one crazed Indian. That man was Sundance.

LASSITER
Jack Slade

Lassiter wasn't the kind of man to listen to reason. Cross him once and he'll hold a grudge for years to come — if he let you live that long.

LAST STAGE TO GOMORRAH
Barry Cord

Jeff Carter, tough ex-riverboat gambler, now had himself a horse ranch that kept him free from gunfights and card games. Until Sturvesant of Wells Fargo showed up.

McALLISTER ON THE COMANCHE CROSSING
Matt Chisholm

The Comanche, McAllister owes them a life — and the trail is soaked with the blood of the men who had tried to outrun them before.

QUICK-TRIGGER COUNTRY
Clem Colt

Turkey Red hooked up with Curly Bill Graham's outlaw crew. But wholesale murder was out of Turk's line, so when range war flared he bucked the whole border gang alone . . .

CAMPAIGNING
Jim Miller

Ambushed on the Santa Fe trail, Sean Callahan is saved by two Indian strangers. But there'll be more lead and arrows flying before the band join Kit Carson against the Comanches.

GUNSLINGER'S RANGE
Jackson Cole

Three escaped convicts are out for revenge. They won't rest until they put a bullet through the head of the dirty snake who locked them behind bars.

RUSTLER'S TRAIL
Lee Floren

Jim Carlin knew he would have to stand up and fight because he had staked his claim right in the middle of Big Ike Outland's best grass.

THE TRUTH ABOUT SNAKE RIDGE
Marshall Grover

The troubleshooters came to San Cristobal to help the needy. For Larry and Stretch the turmoil began with a brawl and then an ambush.

WOLF DOG RANGE
Lee Floren

Will Ardery would stop at nothing, unless something stopped him first — like a bullet from Pete Manly's gun.

DEVIL'S DINERO
Marshall Grover

Plagued by remorse, a rich old reprobate hired the Texas Trouble-shooters to deliver a fortune in greenbacks to each of his victims.

GUNS OF FURY
Ernest Haycox

Dane Starr, alias Dan Smith, wanted to close the door on his past and hang up his guns, but people wouldn't let him.

DONOVAN
Elmer Kelton

Donovan was supposed to be dead. Uncle Joe Vickers had fired off both barrels of a shotgun into the vicious outlaw's face as he was escaping from jail. Now Uncle Joe had been shot — in just the same way.

CODE OF THE GUN
Gordon D. Shirreffs

MacLean came riding home, with saddle tramp written all over him, but sewn in his shirt-lining was an Arizona Ranger's star.

GAMBLER'S GUN LUCK
Brett Austen

Gamblers seldom live long. Parker was a hell of a gambler. It was his life — or his death . . .

ORPHAN'S PREFERRED
Jim Miller

Sean Callahan answers the call of the Pony Express and fights Indians and outlaws to get the mail through.

DAY OF THE BUZZARD
T. V. Olsen

All Val Penmark cared about was getting the men who killed his wife.

THE MANHUNTER
Gordon D. Shirreffs

Lee Kershaw knew that every Rurale in the territory was on the lookout for him. But the offer of $5,000 in gold to find five small pieces of leather was too good to turn down.